LYNSEY STEVENS

lingering embers

Harlequin Books

TORONTO • NEW YORK • LONDON
AMSTERDAM • PARIS • SYDNEY • HAMBURG
STOCKHOLM • ATHENS • TOKYO • MILAN

Harlequin Presents first edition March 1985
ISBN 0-373-10774-9

Original hardcover edition published in 1984
by Mills & Boon Limited

CHAPTER ONE

'No way, Yvie. No way at all!' Dan Kirkoff threw a manuscript on top of a pile of others that awaited his attention.

'But I'm overdue for my vacation now and, well, it is only two weeks when all's said and done.' Yvie heard a note of pleading creep into her voice. 'I'm giving you a month's notice. It's not as though I'm asking for time off tomorrow.'

'Until last night I would have given it to you tomorrow but that's out now, too.' Dan wiped a pudgy hand along the side of his head flattening back his fringe of thin greying hair.

'Dan, I feel I really need this time off,' Yvie appealed to her boss, a man she'd grown to look upon as an especially good friend.

'And four weeks after the date you've asked for, it's yours.' He shoved a long cigarette into the corner of his mouth and flicked his lighter to the tip. 'From the eighteenth, to be precise.'

'Dan——'

'Look, Yvie, you know how important this tour is and I wouldn't be asking you to handle it if I didn't think it needed your touch. Damn it all, girl, what have you got against him? He's a countryman of yours.'

Yvie sighed heavily at a common misapprehension. 'He's English and I'm Australian. There's half a world of difference.'

'Well, you know what I mean. He spent a few years in Australia, didn't he, so that should give you something in common?'

Something in common! Yvie bit back an hysterical laugh. Something in common. A tiny pain began to gnaw away inside her and she felt her whole body begin the familiar tensing. Something in common. Oh, Dan. If only you knew.

'Why can't Paul handle it? Or Abby? They're both more than capable,' she suggested, her voice tight.

'Because I want *you* to handle it, goddamn it!' Dan thumped his open palm on the desk. 'If I'd wanted Abby or Paul to do it I'd have asked them. Now I'm telling you, Yvie, you handle the whole setup. Is that clear?'

Yvie didn't answer. Her throat was closed on a knot of unshed tears and her eyes felt strained and gritty, a legacy of the number of sleepless nights she'd spent since Dan had mentioned his name three weeks ago. Of course, she'd known that the U.S. tour was in the pipeline way back in January but she'd thought, she'd hoped desperately, that it was all just plain rumours. And should it eventuate then she would escape on her vacation. Now the tour was an actuality and the door to her evasion had been firmly closed.

Why the hell couldn't he have changed to another publishing house when his had merged with Dan's firm last year? The merger had come as something of a shock to the industry, more especially to Yvie, although Dan had been beside himself with satisfaction ever since the deal was finalised.

'Yvie.' Dan stood up, five foot four in his stockinged feet and almost as wide as he was tall. He walked around his desk and leant back against it. 'Yvie, you know how important this is going to be for us. He's already made his name and he's not a flash in the pan. He's a natural writer. His second and third books have been impossibly better than his first. Hell, you've read them, too.'

Yvie nodded, 'No one could disagree with that, Dan.'

'Right. And you also know he's only contracted to do one book for us. We don't just want one, we want his next ten, twenty, whatever.'

'I know how important it is to you, Dan. That's just it. I don't think I'm up to coping with it.' She raised her hands in appeal and let them fall. 'I don't want to ruin it for you.'

'That's rubbish, Yvie. You've been here two years and I've yet to see a situation you haven't been able to handle. Why do you think we always call on you to deal with Marge Hazelton?' Dan gave a wry smile as he mentioned their most troublesome writer. 'And there's no comparing him with Marge. From what I've seen so far and heard about him he's as reasonable as they come.'

She wanted to scream at him, *I don't care how reasonable he is! I don't want to do this. I don't want to see him, be near him, hear his voice. I never wanted to, ever again.*

Yvie's heartbeats stumbled agitatedly in her breast. Hadn't she made a new life for herself, put the old one and all its pain behind her, uprooted herself from her home, her country, and travelled around the world to begin again?

'Yvie!' Dan's voice was sharp. 'Have you heard a damn word I've said?'

'I'm sorry, Dan. I——'

'Look, what is it with you, Yvie? You haven't been yourself for days now I come to think of it.' He frowned across at her. 'Perhaps you should go see a doctor. Maybe you're coming down with that flu bug that's going around.' He slapped his forehead theatrically. 'You with flu just at this moment I don't need.'

'I'm not sick, Dan,' she said quietly. 'Just tired.'

'Well, you've got tonight to rest up because I want you bright-eyed tomorrow.' He exhaled a fog of cigarette smoke. 'You want people should think I overwork the best assistant I ever had?'

Yvie smiled and shook her head.

'Right. And we'll have no more talk of time off until this tour's behind us. Okay?'

'Okay.' Yvie sighed faintly.

'Good girl.' Dan went back behind his desk and sat down.

'I'll get back to work then.' Yvie made to leave the office thinking at least she had the better part of a month to psyche herself up for the whole dreadful affair.

'Don't overdo it now,' quipped Dan. 'I want that pretty face all glowing tomorrow night.'

'Tomorrow night?' Yvie paused, her hand on the doorknob, and she turned back to her boss, a frown of enquiry on her face. 'Have I forgotten something?'

'Didn't I tell you?' It was Dan's turn to frown. 'No, of course I didn't. You sidetracked me with all this vacation talk. Like I said, you've got till tomorrow night to get yourself all prettied up because you're coming with me to the airport to meet them.'

'Them?' Yvie had an overwhelming feeling of foreboding.

'Josh Graham and his son. They're flying in tomorrow night.'

Yvie felt herself pale and for a moment she could only stare at Dan's florid face. 'Tomorrow night? But . . . but why? The tour doesn't begin for another month.'

'He's having trouble getting down to the book he's working on from what I can gather, too many distractions. He wanted to try a fresh environment so I suggested here.'

'You suggested San Francisco?' Yvie was numb all over.

'Where else?' Dan shrugged. 'I offered him my place so they're moving in there. You'll be neighbours.' Dan grinned.

Yvie's fingers gripped the doorknob convulsively as her knees shook beneath her. Neighbours? How could she possibly live so close to Josh Graham? They would be virtually sharing a house for she rented a small studio apartment that Dan had had built into his house for his mother while she was alive. Working with Dan as she did it couldn't have been better but . . . To have to live so close to Josh Graham and his wife and son . . . No! How could Dan ask it of her?

'It couldn't have worked out better,' Dan was saying. 'Janice is spending a couple of months in New York with her mother so I'm moving into the apartment here in the city.'

'But you hate the apartment. You like living at Sausalito so much more,' Yvie began.

'I can make the sacrifice this time,' Dan replied wryly and picked up the nearest manuscript. 'Now, I'll get back to it. I want to get through this stack before lunch.'

There was nothing left to dust in the entire apartment. Yvie stowed her cloth and spray cleaner in the cupboard under the sink and ran her eyes over her now gleaming living room. Not that it had been especially dusty when she started her frenzy of cleaning and polishing. It had simply been something to do to keep her thoughts at bay and she'd been fighting her memories since she came home.

Luckily she'd been so busy since she left Dan's office that morning she hadn't had a moment to mull over anything except her work to hand and the presage of Josh Graham's impending arrival had been a mere nagging ache in the back of her mind. Her hectic afternoon had meant she was late home for Dan had been tied up as well so they'd stopped on the way home for a quick dinner at a fast food restaurant.

Dan hated driving, didn't even own a car, and was perfectly happy to have Yvie drive him to and from the office each day in her small blue Pinto. More often than not he'd sit back and read the newspaper as Yvie headed across the Golden Gate from Sausalito, but at least he gave her a brief résumé of the news as he read it.

Dan's house in picturesque Sausalito was about

two thirds of the way up a hillside and overlooked the bay. On a clear evening Yvie could sit for hours at her living room window just gazing out over the twinkling lights of the city and bridges across the bay.

Until four years ago Dan and Janice, his wife of twenty years had shared the house but at that time they had separated, going through what seemed to Yvie to have been a very amicable and civilised divorce and Janice had taken an apartment in the city closer to her interior decorating office. To Yvie's knowledge her boss and his ex-wife were still the best of friends, at least to all outward appearances.

Bending down Yvie struggled to lift a carton of old newspapers and magazines she'd cleaned out and juggled the carton on her hip as she opened the door leading from her living room into the double garage. Her car looked rather forlorn in the large garage and she dumped the box on the floor ready to be put outside for the trash collector. Besides her Pinto the garage held her small washing machine and drier and some old discarded furniture of Dan's. A flight of stairs led up to the main house.

Yvie shivered in the semi-darkness and walked back into her flat. As flats went it was quite tiny but she liked the secure feeling its cosiness gave her and with Dan in the house above the flat and garage she rarely felt nervous. In the two years she had been here she had added her own little touches to make it home to her.

And until recently she had been thoroughly content with her own company. She had a social life of sorts for she often went to the theatre or dined out with friends from work but she was happy enough to be on her own in her small apartment. Until recently. But then again, until recently she had thought she'd left the past quite safely in Australia. Until recently there hadn't been the threat of Josh Graham's imminent appearance.

She wouldn't think about that. She went through into the small bathroom and pulled off her faded denims and T-shirt. The hot shower soothed her tensed and tired muscles somewhat and she decided to shampoo her shoulder length hair. Activity left little time for thought.

Wrapping herself in a towel she took great pains to blow dry her hair. As she brushed it out she gazed at herself in the mirror, smiling wryly at her reflection. Yvie Dean, not exactly the face that launched a thousand ships. Probably her hair was her best feature she decided, and she supposed she was lucky to some extent for it was easy to manage and fell in natural waves that framed her face, accentuating her high cheekbones and the soft curve of her jaw to her slightly stubborn chin.

In the past four years she'd changed, grown up. How could she help it after what had happened. Only in the last year or so had she felt more like a twenty-two year old and less like an aged automaton.

No, definitely not a raging beauty, she told herself. What she didn't see, or refused to acknowledge was the slightly wistful sadness in her smoky grey eyes, the aura of fragility about her, for she couldn't have endured the agony of the loss upon loss of four years ago without the trauma of it all leaving its mark.

Her figure was much more slender now for she'd shed the faint touch of puppy fat she'd carried in her teens. Now she was very fashionably slender. Skinny, she teased herself as she pulled a wry face. But she did have her share of feminine curves, her small firm breasts, narrow waist and contoured hips suiting most modern fashions. Four years ago she'd been very nicely rounded. Cuddly, he'd called her.

Yvie squeezed her eyes tightly closed and ran her brush heavily through her hair wincing as the bristles scraped her scalp. In a way the physical pain was welcome, far more acceptable than the emotional agony remembering brought. She wouldn't remember one moment of that time.

She wasn't the same person. In those days she'd been innocent, naïve, and blindly trusting, in many ways a child. A child in a woman's body she reminded herself, and the familiar ache she couldn't quell began to grow deep down in the pit of her stomach.

Angry with herself she turned away from the mirror, stripping the towel sarong from around her and padding across to the bathroom to hang it on the rack to dry. Back in the living room she took out a clean nightgown, a favourite, an old red and black striped football shirt of Larry's that she'd started wearing and had somehow forgotten to return. It was far too big and hung almost to her mid-thigh but it was comfortable.

She folded out the bottom of the divan which

served as her bed and glanced at her wristwatch as she picked it up off the coffee table. Was it only eight thirty? She checked her clock radio and sighed. Well, perhaps she'd brew a cup of tea and then have an early night. She'd had little enough sleep lately and God knew she was going to need all her resources tomorrow night to carry off the meeting at the airport.

Setting the electric kettle on the boil she wandered unthinkingly over to the bookshelf. One particular group of three novels seemed to spring out at her and she couldn't prevent herself from reaching out to pull the first one from its place.

The cover was colourful, alive with movement, and she knew the storyline was all the cover design promised. Hadn't it made the best-sellers list in record time for a virtually unknown writer?

Almost fatalistically she opened the back cover and gazed at the crisp black and white photo on the dust jacket. Her heartbeats faltered and then steadied. She'd taught herself to look at that photograph without showing any signs of re-cognition. Any outward signs of recognition. Hadn't she?

A slightly cynical smile lifted the corner of her mouth. Why should she recognise him anyway? For the real Josh Graham was nothing like the man she had thought him to be, the man she had so foolishly, so quickly and so perniciously fallen in love with four years ago. The Josh Graham she thought she knew and the real Josh Graham were poles apart and one of them had never even existed, except in the romantic dreams of a very foolish nineteen year old.

Her eyes skimmed down the printed words. Josh Graham, born in London, an ex-journalist who had always wanted to write, etc., etc. The last line burned up at her, a few simple words that cut into the wall of indifference she had erected between now and yesterday. Mr Graham lives in Devon with his wife and son.

The kettle whistled shrilly and Yvie jumped, the book slipping to the floor. She hastily retrieved it and thrust it back on the shelf before hurrying to see to the kettle. Her tea made she sat down with her hot cup cradled in her hands, her eyes drawn back to the three books on the shelf.

They had all topped the best sellers lists and she had enjoyed them all, read them avidly, telling herself it had nothing to do with the fact that he had written them. Her favourite was his first although she refused to admit that the reason lay in her own closeness to it. He'd been writing it at the time and he had unfolded the plot to her as he was putting it down on paper. She'd been excited, knowing it was going to be a success, and she'd been as elated as he had been as the words flowed from his typing fingers.

Yvie slowly sipped her tea, the warm liquid soothing her somewhat and she drew her legs up under her letting the past flood the present. Like a tide those memories had been pushing for release and she sighed brokenly as they escaped to wash over her. How could they hurt her now? She'd come to terms with it all two years ago when she had finally made the break.

Strangely enough it was through her father that she'd met him. Jim Matthews had been involved in the newspaper business all his life. He'd often laughingly told Yvie that his veins ran pure printing ink instead of blood. A vital man, he was the editor of a rather large daily city newspaper and Yvie knew he was well liked and much respected in the journalist industry.

A career journalist, he'd worked all over the world in his younger days and he hadn't married until his early forties. Tragically he'd lost his wife quite suddenly when Yvie was only five years old and so he had raised her single-handedly, always treating her as a contemporary. He discussed most facets of his work with her and for as long as she could remember she hadn't wanted anything other than journalism as her own career.

And then Jim Matthews had suffered a massive heart attack. Yvie had been shocked to her very core. Her father was so well, so energetic looking, so much younger than his sixty-two years. Suddenly both their lives were radically changed. Although he had recovered from the attack it would be some time, the doctors said, before her father would be able to resume work.

At the time Yvie had been studying journalism at the Queensland Institute of Technology and she'd taken leave of absence from her course to care for her father when he left the hospital. Physically, her father improved, but psychologically his attack had set him back. It took Yvie and the doctors weeks to convince Jim Matthews that his life was not over.

Eventually, Yvie talked him into spending some time recuperating at the beach. They owned a small house at Golden Beach at Caloundra and they'd used it at weekends and for each of Yvie's school vacations. After the first month Jim's improvement was such that they were both in high spirits and life was gradually getting back to normal. In another couple of months Yvie was planning on returning to her studies.

On the morning she met Josh Graham, Yvie and her father had had their early morning swim in the sea and the water had been so warm and invigorating that Yvie had stayed a little longer while her father returned to the house to shower and change. Eventually she reluctantly walked out of the surf and up the beach to the house. As she approached the small cottage she'd heard voices. Thinking it was their milkman, who often stopped to chat to her father, she'd washed the sand from her bare feet at the tap and climbed the three steps on to the patio.

With her towel slung carelessly over her shoulder she'd strolled casually into the kitchen, stopping midstride in the doorway, her eyes widening in surprise. The stranger lounging back against the kitchen table, his arms folded across his chest, was definitely not the milkman. Who could he be?

He was dressed in blue scrub denims and a short sleeved pale blue and white pin-striped shirt, the colour suiting his fair colouring. His blond hair was short in the front and styled to the shape of his head at the back, almost reaching his collar, and his eyes were a mid blue.

Too good looking, Yvie thought, her eyes on his profile. Blond, blue-eyed and probably a regular bighead.

He sensed her presence immediately and turned slightly, his eyes taking her in in one bold glance before slowly making a more detailed inspection, running over her legs and upwards.

Suddenly her modest bikini was far too brief. Yvie felt herself begin to blush. Her eyes fell from his in an unaccustomed embarrassment and she chastised herself. What was the matter with her? She'd never before felt so young ... so inexperienced.

'Ah, Yvie!' Her father turned as he switched off the now boiling kettle. 'Come and meet Josh. Josh, my daughter, Yvette. Yvie, this is Josh Graham, a friend of mine. We used to work together.'

Josh Graham inclined his head and stood away from the table. He was all of six foot tall and his broad shoulders tapered to narrow hips and long muscular denim clad legs.

'Hello.' Yvie murmured, her vocal chords stiff and tight.

'Hi! How was the water?' His voice was deep and resonant and a tiny shiver of pleasure began deep in the pit of her stomach, spiralling upwards. He had a slightly British accent and when he smiled Yvie literally felt her knees turn to water.

'Fine. The water was fine. Dad and I swim every morning,' she got out in a breathless rush.

'Yes, she's something of a slavedriver when it comes to seeing I get my exercise,' laughed her father who, although he had lost a considerable amount of weight, had regained some of his colour. 'Drags me into the surf every morning and I've never been one for the water. Still, they tell me it's good for me.' He winked affectionately at Yvie. 'Come and have a cuppa, love.'

'I'll just go and change first.' The blue eyes ran over her again. 'Excuse me.' Yvie bolted for her room and standing in the middle of the floor she tried to still her fast beating heart.

It had to have been the surprise. Yes, coming in to the kitchen and seeing him unexpectedly standing there when she had surmised her father was talking to the friendly milkman. It was simply that she'd been taken unawares. Why else would she have lost her composure? Men had never effected her that way.

Since her mother's death there had only been Yvie and her father and if Jim Matthews' attitude of always treating his daughter as a person in her own right had done one thing it had ensured that she was at home in any company. She always felt herself capable of handling any situation. Usually she was as at her ease with men, even those of her father's vintage, as she was with women. But there was something different about Josh Graham, some indefinable magnetism that had her heart fluttering in her breast like a trapped bird.

Mentally shaking herself Yvie walked across to her duchess and selected some fresh underclothes. She was being over imaginative. After all she was a normal, fairly well adjusted and, she would have said grown up, nineteen year old. She'd never lacked for dates and besides, there was Larry, who she guessed could be called her steady. They'd known each other for years and when he'd last had leave from the Navy their relationship had undergone a slightly perceptible change. She knew Larry wanted them to be closer.

She picked up her denim shorts and a loose fitting T-shirt and hurried into the shower. After washing the salt water out of her hair and from her body she vigorously towelled herself dry and pulled on her clothes. Catching sight of herself in the mirror she grimaced.

Unfashionably lumpy she described herself somewhat supercritically. Yvie rested her hands on her hips and surveyed herself. Her narrow waist only seemed to emphasise her rounded hips and full breasts and a small frown puckered her brow. She'd have to try dieting, she decided as she picked up her brush and tugged it through the damp short tendrils.

Now that she'd restored some order to her hair there was nothing left to keep her in her room. She could delay joining her father and the compelling Josh Graham no longer. Yvie took a deep breath and trod reluctantly along the passage to the kitchen.

Josh Graham was seated now, across from Yvie's father, and she stepped a little breathlessly up to the table.

'That's the longest shower I've known you take, love,' laughed Jim Matthews. 'I poured your tea so it's probably cold.'

Yvie cupped the pottery mug in her hands. 'It's okay,' she said and raised the drink to her lips. It could have been dishwater for all she tasted it.

Josh Graham's blue eyes followed her movements and the mug shook slightly in her hands.

He took a sip of his own tea and Yvie was as mesmerised by his movements as he had seemed to be by hers. His lips touched on the rim of the mug and the muscles in his throat moved as he swallowed.

A tremor of excitant awareness quivered down the length of Yvie's spine and she shifted in her chair, her heartbeats catching in her chest, restricting her breathing. She set her mug down and clasped her trembling hands together in her lap.

Fixing her gaze on the cross stitched pattern on the checked gingham tablecloth she willed herself to take slow even breaths. Her father was speaking, telling Josh Graham about the fish he'd caught the evening before and Yvie forced her numbed senses to concentrate on what her father was saying. But she was powerless to stop her eyes darting small all-encompassing glances across at Josh Graham.

He really was fantastic looking, not as pretty-boy as she had at first thought, for his nose had the sign of a distinct break and his jaw was perhaps a little too square, too rugged to be described as 'chocolate box'. More, he was compelling, the type of man who would rate and receive a second look in a crowd.

While Yvie sat in silence her father and Josh Graham discussed various workmates they'd had in common and then the last assignment Josh had worked on in South East Asia. His brow clouded as he spoke of the squalor, the suffering and Yvie found herself hanging on his every word, caught up neatly in the web of his magnetism. Jim Matthews nodded. He'd found much the same conditions himself years ago.

They moved on to less disturbing subjects and Josh mentioned that he was visiting friends for the weekend. He was looking for somewhere to stay for a couple of months, somewhere quiet, where he could work.

'I've finished up as a journalist, at least for a time.' Josh drained his mug. 'I've decided to give the novel I've always wanted to write a try.' He smiled wrly. 'I've been promising myself the chance for years.'

'You have to make up your mind and do it.' Jim agreed. 'For the past twenty years I was going to try a novel myself but I always put it off.'

Yvie glanced at her father in surprise and he smiled ruefully.

'And now here I am still just thinking about it. You're taking a positive step.'

'If it comes to nothing at least I'll have given myself the opportunity.' Josh shrugged. 'I was due for leave anyway so I'll give myself a couple of months up here and see how it goes. The unit I've rented isn't far down the beach from your place.'

It wasn't far. Only a short walk. It had only taken Yvie minutes to reach him . . .

Yvie stood up quickly, stopping her memories with the activity, and she crossed to tip what was left of her tea down the sink. Mulling it all over wasn't going to help the situation at all.

So she'd found him attractive. So what? So had plenty of other females she had no doubt. Well, she was now four years older, four years wiser, and there was no way she was going to allow history to repeat itself.

Resolutely she climbed into bed. The past was in the past and it was going to stay there. And what makes you think Josh Graham will even be interested in wanting to turn back the clock? She asked herself tortuously. What makes you think Josh Graham will even remember you?

That thought pushed the peaceful oblivion of sleep even further from her mind.

CHAPTER TWO

THE airport was its usual teeming self, people hurrying every which way, some striding purposefully, others struggling with cumbersome luggage.

'At least we don't have long to wait. The plane's already landed according to that monitor over there,' remarked Dan, who hated airports.

Usually Yvie loved them, could feel the excitement of imminent departure, the happiness of homecoming.

'Hope they don't get held up in customs. That'd be the pits.' Dan shifted irritatedly in the protesting moulded seat.

Sitting beside Dan Yvie took a deep steadying breath as her heartbeats began to race again. Don't break down now, she ordered herself forcefully. You've been as cool as a cucumber all day. But that had been today, today with only the threat of the arrival of evening. Now it was here. The time had come. Yvie suppressed an hysterical urge to giggle. She sounded like the voice of doom. Your time is at hand.

'Want some coffee?' Dan asked desultorily, breaking into her agitated thoughts.

'No, thanks.' Yvie shook her head, her fingers playing nervously with the strap of her shoulder bag.

'You look a little pale. You okay?' Dan frowned at her.

'Yes, I'm fine.'

'Good.' Dan glanced at his wristwatch. 'Surely they'd be through customs by now,' he grumbled but Yvie was scarcely listening.

Her breath had caught in her throat and she was certain her heart had momentarily ceased beating. He was just as she remembered him. Tall, broad and fair haired. And every bit as compellingly attractive.

Taking a deep steadying breath Yvie used all her faltering willpower to keep her face devoid of expression. She was indifferent to him, she told herself vehemently. All feeling for him had died, painfully, and she would never be vulnerable to him again. No man, most especially Josh Graham, was ever going to get so close again.

He strode towards them, long legs eating up the distance between them, a man exuding confidence, so very sure of himself, and Yvie had to choke back the cry of outrage that fought to burst from her. He'd been just as self-possessed back then. He'd been aware of the effect he had on her and he'd used it to overcome her youthful reticence with almost indecent ease. She'd fallen head over heels in love with him practically from the moment she saw him. How quickly he'd come to mean her world to her.

Yvie calmed herself again with no little difficulty. There was no point in rehashing all that right now. It was in the past, that supposedly undying love, that all consuming fire. It was dead and buried. Josh Graham had given it life and just as easily destroyed it.

Her eyes met his as those long legs propelled

him closer and she refused to let her level gaze fall. She held his gaze unwaveringly. He spared one swift glance for Dan but his eyes returned immediately to Yvie, their expression inscrutable.

But there was no surprise at seeing her in their blue depths, Yvie realised. There was recognition. She could see he remembered her but he wasn't at all taken aback that she should be here. In fact she knew instinctively that he had been expecting her. Shock reverberated about inside her. He'd known. But how?

Her lips parted and something flickered for one brief second in his eyes before his lids and his long lashes, dark for one so fair, fell to shield his expression. He stopped and then he was turning away from her, his hand going out to Dan.

'Dan Kirkoff? Pleased to meet you at last.' He smiled as the two men shook hands and Yvie's knuckles turned white where her hands clutched her shoulder bag.

'Josh. You, too,' Dan beamed like a benevolent koala bear. He turned to Yvie. 'And meet my assistant, Yvie Dean. She'll be at your disposal, to show you around, smooth the way for you, and she'll be in charge of your tour when the time comes. Yvie's our best.'

Yvie didn't extend her hand to him. There was no way she was going to touch him ever again. She nodded slightly with hard-won outward calmness.

'How do you do.' Yes, she'd managed to keep her voice reasonably steady. She had everything under control.

Josh inclined his head in return, one corner of his mouth lifting in a faintly cynical smile.

'Pleased to meet you,' he paused distinctly, 'Mrs Dean.'

Yvie's eyes flew to his. Was there mockery there in their blue depths? But his expression once again gave no indication of his thoughts. Had there been some message in the tone of his voice? Mrs Dean. So he knew that, too. How much more had he found out?

No! He couldn't have discovered . . .

Now Josh had drawn a young boy forward, a youngster with a slightly sullen droop to his boyish mouth.

'This is my son, Tim,' he said.

The youngster held out his hand to Dan obediently enough, surprisingly conducting himself with an assurance far beyond his years.

He must be what? Twelve, Yvie reckoned, so he was quite tall for his age, at least as tall as she was, and his youthful face promised to be as handsome as his father's. His hair was fair like Josh's but where his father's was relatively straight Tim's was a mass of loose curls.

'Hi!' A little hesitantly Tim smiled at Yvie with Josh's eyes and something caught at her so that her own smile felt stiff and forced.

'Hello. Did you enjoy your flight?' she asked him uneasily.

'It was a bit long but the movies they showed were great. One was about hang gliders.' He shoved his hands into the back pockets of his faded denims and lapsed into silence, pulling his lips downwards again.

With his denims he wore far from new sneakers and a loose-fitting sweatshirt bearing the garishly iridescent name of what could only be a way out pop group, but with all that unruly hair, Yvie thought wryly, no one could call Tim Graham a punk rocker. He was probably a nice kid when he forgot to be sulky.

'How about the other one?' Yvie prompted and Tim blinked at her. 'The other movie,' she specified.

'Oh. It was "Chariots of Fire".' Tim mumbled and Yvie watched the small frown cloud Josh's brow.

'Well, shall we make a move?' Dan asked glancing around at the trolley of luggage and the attendant skycap.

They all started for the exit through the now thinning mêlée. Dan hailed a waiting taxi.

'We'll take a cab as I didn't think we'd all fit in Yvie's car. Glad we did now,' Dan chuckled as he watched the luggage being juggled into the taxi's large boot.

Tim opened the back door and climbed inside, sliding across to the opposite window. Before Yvie could make a move Dan had seated himself in the front by the driver. Josh's hand reached out to the open back door of the car and he stood silently waiting for Yvie to get in. Yvie slid inside feeling him follow her.

Before she had a chance to move he was beside her, his thigh touching hers, his arm brushing her arm. Panic-stricken she slid away from him, only to come up against Tim who folded his arms and slouched down in the seat. Yvie slowly exhaled her trapped breath and inched back towards the centre of the seat to give Tim a little more room.

Besides, there was no way she was going to let Josh Graham know that his nearness had any effect on her. Because it didn't. It didn't. Not anymore.

Josh's leg, clad in tailored grey slacks touched Yvie's thigh again and involuntarily she tried to compact herself into the smallest possible space she could manage. The material of his slacks seemed to Yvie to rasp loudly against the soft jersey of her skirt and she could feel the tension gripping her, rising to almost choke her. Her fingers fiddled with her blouse, firstly with the buttons and then with the loose bow tie neckline. Her neck began to ache from holding herself rigidly upright, to avoid touching him.

Now the taxi driver began to weave expertly through the freeway traffic and Yvie was swayed towards Josh until their shoulders touched. The sleeve of his pale blue body shirt was soft, almost caressing, on the bare skin of her arm. Her senses were reeling, her heartbeats thudding loudly in her throat.

The taxi swerved and the driver swore under his breath, tooting his horn in retaliation. Yvie was thrown solidly against Josh and his hand went to her bare arm to steady her, his knuckles brushing the side of her breast. She pulled away from him as though she had been stung and she felt his sharp glance. She turned away, glad of the dimness of the car's interior that cloaked her overheated cheeks. She burned all over, the imprint of his touch on her searing, radiating from the points of contact to every last inch of her body. Reaching out she clasped the back of the front seat to steady herself. She mustn't touch him, have him touch her.

'Is it far?' Tim asked from beside her making her realise she was all but wedged up against him.

'A fair way. Another fifteen minutes or so I'd say.' She tried valiantly to relax.

'We're heading for my apartment,' put in Dan from the front, turning slightly in his seat so that he could talk to them. 'I'll get off there and then Yvie will be driving you over to Sausalito in her car.'

'We can catch a cab to the house and save you the trip,' Josh said and Dan laughed.

'It's no trouble, Yvie's going your way. She lives over there, too.'

'I see.' Josh's eyes were on her again, Yvie could feel them.

'Works in pretty well actually,' Dan continued. 'Yvie usually chauffeurs me to and from the office each day so it's very convenient.'

'Are you Mr Kirkoff's personal secretary?' Tim asked.

'More like my Girl Friday,' Dan chuckled before Yvie could reply. 'And a prettier one would be hard to find. Yvie's a little treasure, aren't you, love?'

'If you say so, Dan.' Yvie managed to keep her voice light.

'How long have you worked for Dan, Yvie?' Josh's deep voice asked.

'Two years,' she replied flatly.

'Yvie worked for a friend of mine in Australia and when he heard I needed an assistant he recommended Yvie for the position. Best favour he's ever done me.'

'What made you want to work in the States?' Josh enquired with seeming casualness.

Yvie shrugged. 'I felt I needed a change of scene.'

'And it's all worked out great,' beamed Dan. 'This little lady's the tops.'

'That's some praise from your boss,' Josh said beside her. 'I'm glad you'll be handling the tour.' His tone had dropped slightly, it's depth striking chords way deep in her memory but she shut them off before they could escape to twist inside her.

They were in the city proper now and it didn't take long to reach Dan's ex-wife's apartment. Dan directed the driver to the underground car park and they pulled up beside Yvie's Pinto. The luggage went from one boot to the other with Josh's typewriter and Tim's kitbag being stowed on the back seat. Tim climbed into the back and arranged the luggage around him.

'Well, Josh, it's been a pleasure meeting you.' Dan had paid the taxi fare and turned back to the other man. 'I hope you don't mind if Yvie escorts you the rest of the way.'

Josh's eyes skimmed lightly over Yvie as she stood beside the car willing the drive to be over and done with.

'Not at all.' He smiled and Dan chuckled.

'A man would be mad, wouldn't he.'

They were chatting as though she wasn't there, fumed Yvie, and she turned and slid behind the wheel. If Josh Graham didn't get into the car in a hurry she'd leave without him.

He shook hands with Dan and strode easily

around to the passenger side. He fumbled beneath the seat and slid it back to its maximum and even then his long legs seemed cramped.

Too bad, thought Yvie ungraciously. This car suited her fine.

'See you in the morning, love,' Dan waved as she backed expertly between a post and a long American sedan.

Fortunately the traffic took the majority of her concentration and she only spoke to point out various landmarks to Tim or to answer one of his queries. Josh remained silent although he looked about him with interest.

Stopped at a red traffic light Yvie's gaze slid over his legs, caught in her peripheral vision and she felt herself stiffening instinctively. She snapped her eyes back to the car in front of her. There was no way she was going to let him get to her again so there would be no more sideways glances, no recognition of his undoubted attractiveness.

'Are we going to cross the Golden Gate?' Tim broke in on her self chastisement as they passed a large road sign.

'Yes. Here it is now. The famous Golden Gate. Would you like me to stop just over the bridge so you can get a better view?'

'Can you? That'd be great, wouldn't it, Dad?'

'If it's no trouble.' Josh turned slightly to look at her.

'No. It's no trouble.' Yvie changed lanes with the air of much practice and pulled off the highway into a parking area.

'This is called Vista Point,' she directed at Tim as they climbed out of the car.

Tim ran across to the safety wall and Yvie walked after him. She didn't wait to see if Josh followed her. She didn't have to for she was dreadfully conscious of him falling in beside her and the cold shiver that passed over her had little to do with the briskness of the breeze that flattened Yvie's skirt against her legs.

It was a clear night with no fog and at any other time Yvie would have been enchanted by the view; the bay, the lights of the city, the threads of headlights crossing the bridges; but tonight her attention was held by other sensations, other awarenesses.

They reached the solid wall, joining Tim, and stood there supposedly gazing at the scene, but Yvie sensed that the panorama held as little of Josh's attention as it held of hers.

'Is that the bridge with two layers of roads?' Tim asked, pointing to the left.

'Yes. The Bay Bridge to Oakland,' Yvie replied. 'I've always thought it was more interesting than the Golden Gate but it's the Golden Gate that holds all the romantic attraction apparently.'

Tim moved further along, away from Yvie and his father, and Yvie's nerve ends tightened again. The silence arched between them, screaming above the whistle of the wind.

'Well, Yvie.' His deep voice startled her. 'So I've found you.'

Her head snapped around so that her eyes met his and the wind whipped her hair across her face. With one slightly unsteady hand she brushed it aside, catching it back behind her ear.

'Found me?' She heard herself repeat his words although she had no conscious recollection of summoning the words.

'Found you,' he concurred.

'Why?' Yvie asked, her throat dry. 'Why could you possibly want to find me?'

'Why indeed.' His eyes bored into hers. 'Why wouldn't I?' he asked softly, his tone sending shivers of that long forgotten awareness along her spine and she was far too late to stop it, to halt that particular re-creation.

'It took me no inconsiderable time,' he continued. 'If I didn't know better I'd have said you were trying to disappear.'

'Trying to—— But that's ridiculous. I told you why I came to the States, for a change of scene. My reasons had nothing to do with wanting to disappear. Why would I want to do that?'

Josh's eyes sparkled in the dusky light.

'I simply wanted a change of scene,' Yvie repeated. 'Is that too much to believe?'

There was a moment's silence.

'I guess not.' Josh rubbed the back of his neck as though to ease his tension. 'But trying to find you brought me up against nothing but brick walls.' He paused. 'I was sorry to hear of your father's death. I wouldn't have even known about it if I hadn't been looking for you. Was it his heart?'

Yvie nodded. 'I don't think he ever really got over the first attack.'

'No one I spoke to seemed to know what happened to you after your father died. Someone said they'd heard you'd moved to Sydney, someone else thought New Zealand. I was at a dead end until my publishing house merged with Dan Kirkoff's. And then I only heard of you by a great stroke of luck. Dan himself mentioned you once on the phone and I took it from there. I remember once you said you'd like to get into publishing and Yvie's not such a common name, although I was looking for an Yvie Matthews, not a Mrs Yvie Dean.'

Yvie could feel the tension in his whole stance without even looking at him and her heartbeats fluttered nervously. How she wished Tim would rejoin them but he was metres away from them, seemingly still engrossed in the view.

'Is he an American?' Josh's voice was taut.

'Who?' Yvie played for time, trying to gather her scattered wits about her.

'Your husband,' he barked with restrained harshness, irritation in every shadowed line of his body.

'No. Australian,' Yvie said hesitantly. 'I think . . . you met him once.'

'I met him?' His head came up.

'Yes. At the coast. Larry. Larry Dean.' Her words tumbled out. 'He came home one weekend on leave from the Navy.'

That weekend came rushing back with amazing ease, its clarity shocking her. She could almost taste the frustration of having to share Josh's hours with Larry and she could feel the weight of her guilt because each moment she spent with Larry she so desperately wanted to be with Josh. Only Josh.

'The sailor?' Josh's tone barely stopped short of being derogatory and Yvie felt a wave of anger rise within her, anger on Larry's behalf, anger with herself because she still carried that remembered guilt.

'Yes, the sailor,' she said curtly. 'Larry asked me to marry him and I did.'

'Why did you?' The words seemed to be torn out of him.

'Because I...' Yvie took a gulping breath. Because I loved him. She could almost laugh at that. It would be a blatant lie because she hadn't loved Larry the way a woman should love the man she marries. She had only loved one man like that and he had betrayed that love.

Yvie shrugged her shoulder with as much flippancy as she could manage. 'Why shouldn't I have married Larry? I'd known him for years, since we were school children in fact, and besides, he looked very dashing in his uniform. What girl wouldn't have been impressed?'

Josh held her gaze for long seconds before he swung away, his back to her tense and straight, his hands clasping the rough surfaced parapet.

'Look at the marina down there, Dad.' Tim bounded back to them. 'Can you see it?'

Josh stepped across to his son, leaving Yvie standing apart, to watch them, fighting a pain that plunged deep inside her. She clenched her hands in the pockets of her skirt and tried to tell herself that it was over, that the pain was for the past, that it had nothing whatsoever to do with now. Nothing whatsoever to do with Josh Graham being here.

After a moment they all moved back to the car. Josh slid silently into the seat beside her and Yvie switched on the ignition and shifted the gearlever into place with a faint crunch.

The tension inside the car had multiplied threefold as Yvie pulled out into the stream of traffic and put her foot down on the accelerator, only wanting to get home, to find sanctuary in her flat, to escape the volatile strain of Josh's nearness. The tires screeched protestingly as she flung the car around a corner and she saw Josh shift his feet beside her, bracing himself.

Forcing herself to relax her grip on the steering wheel Yvie eased her foot off the accelerator. There was no point in doing them all bodily harm. She just had to remain calm, keep the whole thing in perspective. She mustn't get involved in the situation. She mustn't let him get close.

So he had found her, as he put it. Well, now he'd know it was a lost cause. She had been lost to him four years ago.

Found her. The words reverberated about inside her. She felt a tiny frown cloud her brow as she drove the car up the familiar circuitous road. Why had he wanted to find her? What possible reason could have made him come in search of her? Surely not because he still cared? No! No, he was the one who had broken up their relationship, their affair, she reminded herself brutally.

And knowing how much pain that last time had brought her she had no intention of allowing it all to start again. She'd go to any lengths to protect

herself, use any means to hold him at arm's
length.

An overhead street light caught and ricocheted
off the thick gold band set with four tiny
sapphires that she wore on her left hand. She
hadn't taken it off, although she refused to
acknowledge what she faintly suspected, that she
used Larry's wedding band as some kind of
protection.

Well, protection was what she wanted now and
she'd even go so far as to use Larry as a barrier
against Josh Graham. If Josh thought her to be a
happily married woman then surely he . . . She
broke off that train of thought and almost
laughed cynically. He had no ideals about the
sanctity of marriage. Hadn't he only used his own
when he wanted out? Well, two could play at that
game. Only this time she'd be using her marriage
to keep him out.

She turned the car into the steep driveway and
pushed the button on the remote control that sent
the garage door swinging upwards. She accelerated into the garage.

'Hey, that's neat.' Tim grinned as she pulled
up and Yvie smiled involuntarily. 'Is this where
we're staying?'

'Yes, this is Dan's house.' Yvie opened her
door.

'Where do you live?' Tim climbed out after
her. 'Somewhere nearby?'

'I live here too,' she said evenly and her eyes
met Josh's across the top of the car.

CHAPTER THREE

Yvie sighed heavily and cast her magazine aside. She couldn't seem to concentrate on a fashion magazine tonight and she was far too hyped up to sleep. Her eyes went to the ceiling of her flat. Above her Josh Graham and his son, Tim, were settling themselves in to Dan's house, just the thickness of the building materials away.

She'd taken them upstairs when they arrived and handed Josh the keys. Her tour of the house had been perfunctory to say the least but by then she'd simply wanted to escape from Josh's presence. And so she'd left them to return to her own flat mouthing the words that should they need anything she was below and to feel free to call on her.

Yvie grimaced. What an out and out piece of hypocrisy that had been. If she had her way she'd never see Josh Graham again. And that was a fact.

The same tiny tingle of awareness teased the pit of her stomach as his face swam unbidden before her. Yvie sprang out of her chair and prowled agitatedly about her living room. She laced her fingers through her hair and then massaged her throbbing temples with her fingertips. This was ridiculous. Here she was falling apart and he'd only just arrived. She had to face a month and then a hectic tour with him. She'd have to pull herself together.

All at once the flat was stifling and she pulled the top of her fleecy lined grey tracksuit over her head and opened the glass sliding door that gave on to her own small patio. At least Yvie called it her patio. Rather it was a small section of the garden in front of her flat that had been cobbled and when the weather was warm enough she sat out in the sun on her lounger reading or simply relaxed soaking up the sunshine.

The breeze had freshened and lifted her hair back from her face. Yvie thrust her hands into the front pockets of her tracksuit top and she shivered not unpleasantly. Already the wind was unravelling the cobwebs in her mind.

What a disaster the evening had been. She'd planned on being distantly cool but when it had come to the crunch had she been as cool as she thought she was? Her lip twisted cynically as she admitted her outward composure had been harder to maintain than she would have thought possible.

Josh Graham's face conjured itself in her mind's eye again. No, he hadn't changed, not one little bit. He didn't appear to be even noticeably older. If possible he was more devastatingly attractive than he'd been four years ago. There. She'd admitted it.

And what about herself? Did he see the change in her? Because she had changed. Did he find her as attractive as he undeniably had four years ago? She shivered as the thought triggered off an uncontrollable tide of wanting.

So much for the cool calm touch-me-not façade. It appeared it was as brittle and thin as an egg shell, and as easily fractured. Her fingers clenched into fists within the warmth of the pockets of her tracksuit top. Trying to relax she leant back against the small patio table one ankle crossed over the other, and her eyes absently followed the lights flickering on the bay.

Yes, Josh Graham was as attractive to her as he'd always been. From the moment she'd met him. And suddenly she was back in the kitchen of their beach house, sitting at the table opposite her father and Josh Graham, and they'd just met. Her father left the room to get some newspapers clippings to show Josh and they were there together. Alone. But that was nothing new. It seemed they had existed in a world of their own from the moment their eyes had first met.

Yvie fiddled with her teaspoon until eventually her gaze was drawn to his, read the obviously sensual message in their blue depths. He was interested in her, she'd have had to have been blind not to see that, and she knew just as surely that the feelings were reciprocated. The gathering excitement that knowledge brought shocked her for she'd never experienced a feeling quite like it before. There was something different about Josh Graham, something she couldn't at that moment define, but she knew her meeting with him held all the excitement of a beginning, a sail through uncharted waters as dangerous as they were provocatively unknown.

They talked, although she couldn't recall what they said, but their spoken words couldn't have matched the conversation they were holding with their eyes. And when he left them to drive back to his friends he left her feeling empty and somehow adrift.

She should have drawn the line right there, Yvie told herself, but it was so easy to say from four years on. One could be extremely sensible with hindsight. However, for a nineteen year old who had never known any man as attractive, as blatantly arresting as Josh Graham, to walk away at that moment hadn't even seemed a possibility.

A match rasped and flared off to her right and Yvie smothered a cry, momentarily frozen as a rush of gruesome stories flashed through her mind, stories of violence one could read in the newspapers every day, of women caught alone. Her body tensed for flight.

'It's only me.' He stepped into the pool of light filtering through the open curtains of her living-room.

A wave of relief was followed by a renewed, totally different type of tension as Yvie stood looking at him.

'I'm sorry if I startled you. I didn't realise you were there until a moment ago.' He drew on his cigarette and exhaled slowly.

Yvie glanced from him to the house. 'I thought you'd have been in bed suffering from jet lag.' Her voice was tight and sounded short and almost rude.

'Hasn't caught up with me yet,' he replied easily, 'but Tim's dead to the world.'

Yvie dragged her eyes away from him to gaze once more over the night lights of San Francisco.

'Spectacular view,' he remarked and Yvie could only nod. Her tension increased as she instinctively felt him move closer.

'Yvie?' His tone was low and husky, reaching out to envelop her in a stimulating cloak of a desire she suddenly remembered far too well. Slowly she turned her head to look at him.

'I can't believe I've found you at last,' he continued softly. 'There hasn't been a day in the past four years when I haven't thought of you, wondered where you were, what you were doing.'

Hope sprang unbidden inside Yvie and she quickly quelled it. But not swiftly enough. For one indescribable moment she knew an urge to forget the past, forget his betrayal, and just throw herself into his arms, feel them bind her to him, his heartbeats quickening beneath her fingers resting on the solid strength of his chest.

She levered herself away from the patio table and put space between them. 'Now, Josh, that's a little hard to believe after all this time,' she finished with a forced laugh.

'But true,' he said, his words harsher, less sensual. 'When we parted I needed time to get everything sorted out. I had a son I barely knew because my job kept me away from home. I had a marriage that was no marriage at all. I needed to get my life into order before you and I——'

'I considered our parting to be extremely final,' Yvie cut in, not wanting to listen to his words, for that's all they were, words trying to make up for years of pain. 'Now I'm cold and I'm going inside.'

Yvie strode over to the sliding glass door and her hand reached out for the catch.

'Yvie, I have to talk to you.' Josh followed her until he was standing beside her, his hand reaching out to halt her but she evaded his restraining touch, sliding the door open and stepping inside.

He was just as quick to step in behind her and, his eyes not leaving her, he slid the door closed behind him, shutting out the chilly moonlit night.

They stood looking at each other for long stretched seconds and then Josh relaxed, leaning back against the door his gaze moving about her small flat until eventually his eyes came back to her face.

Yvie swallowed painfully, her eyes warring with his. 'There's a door through there to the garage.' She indicated pointedly with a movement of her head.

'We have to talk,' he repeated not making any move to leave her.

'It's late, Josh, and I'm working tomorrow. Besides, I don't really think we have anything to talk about.'

'I would have said we did, that we had more than enough to talk about.' He gazed at her intently. 'You're part of my past, Yvie, and you've always been present in part of my heart. You must have known that, even then.'

'Did I? You're wrong about that, Josh,' Yvie said flatly. 'I'd say you did a pretty good job of cutting me out of your life. So why don't we just leave it at that.'

'But you must have understood the situation——'

'Oh, I understood it very well and you were right to call it quits when you did, before we got in any deeper.' A sharp pain stabbed at her heart but she forced the memory back, back into the depths of yesterday. 'Let's just say that we did the sensible thing.'

'I thought you appreciated the position I was in,' Josh's eyes glowed icily.

Yvie shrugged. 'It's four years later and we're both four years older. We can't turn back the clock.'

His eyes still held hers compellingly. 'I loved you more than life itself.'

Yvie's heartbeats caught in her chest and she fought for breath, a dull flush climbing her cheeks.

'But I had . . . my responsibilities lay with Tim. Surely you must have seen that?'

'Josh, let's leave it. It's old news. Why rake it all up again?' Yvie ran a distracted hand through her hair. 'It's been a long day and I'm tired. Please go.'

He walked towards her and Yvie stepped automatically backwards.

'Yvie.' His hand reached out towards her and she lunged away from him.

'Don't touch me!' The words burst from her and Josh lifted his head like a wild beast taking a scent.

The backs of Yvie's legs were against the divan and she watched helplessly as he took the step that brought him mere inches from her.

'Josh, as far as I'm concerned you said everything that needed to be said four years ago.'

His hands reached out, clasped her arms, his fingers firm, sending shivers of that old elation surging through her.

'Let me go!' She pushed her hands against the wall of his chest, exerting every ounce of her willpower against the shaft of desire that urged her to capitulate, to relax, to rest her body breathtakingly on his, to know again the delight of experiencing the length of him moving with her.

'Yvie!'

The battle raged within her as she fought the assault of his potent nearness on her painfully constructed defences.

'Josh, I'm not going to let you pick up where you left off. I'm a totally different person now, not the silly, easily impressed juvenile I used to be.'

'You were never that, Yvie, and you know it. You were never anything other than a total woman. Not to me.' His voice slid sensuously lower and his fingers moved caressingly over her arms as though he couldn't help himself.

To her heightened awareness his skin seemed to abrade loudly on the soft material of her tracksuit. His head had begun the descent, his lips curving softly, seeking her mouth.

She turned her head abruptly away. 'No, Josh!'

'Why?' The word burst brutally out of him.

'Because I don't want you to,' she replied harshly. 'I would have thought that was fairly obvious.'

His fingers were biting into the flesh of her arms now as he held her for a moment before he broke away from her, turning so that his back was to her, his hands going to his hips, tension in every line of his body.

'Because of your marriage,' he said flatly, a statement rather than a question.

'Wouldn't you say that was a good enough reason?' Yvie asked quietly, pushing away the feeling of loss that washed over her at his releasing her.

Josh walked across to her window and stood gazing out into the night. 'When did you marry him?' he asked, his voice devoid of expression.

'After you left,' Yvie told him with an edge of defiance.

'Where is he now?'

'At sea. He's still in the Navy, working towards becoming an officer.' Yvie swallowed. 'Larry's always been ambitious and he's making the Navy his career.'

Josh met this with silence, resting on his hands on the windowsill.

'Yvie, how could you do it?' His words were tight and forced.

'Do it? My God, Josh, you've got a nerve. You have no right to ask me that, no right at all.' She wrapped her arms protectively around her. 'Now please leave. I see no reason to continue this conversation.'

'Yvie.' His voice was tortured and he started towards her.

'Josh, please.' Yvie held up her hand. 'We're going to have to work together for the next few months. Don't make it any harder than it already is.'

Their eyes met again and held and Yvie's were the first to fall.

'As far as anyone's concerned I'd rather we left

it that we met today. There's no need for anyone to know about—' Yvie faltered and Josh's eyebrow rose mockingly.

'About?'

'That we knew each other before,' Yvie finished lamely.

'Knew each other,' Josh repeated and gave a harsh cynical laugh. 'We more than knew each other, Yvie, you know that. I felt I knew you right to the depths of your soul. As I knew myself. We were one, two halves of one whole.' His eyes raked her. 'But maybe I was wrong,' he finished softly. 'And maybe you're right. Perhaps you are different.'

Yvie felt the pain begin to clutch at her as she watched Josh's broad shoulders seem to sag, all his previous aggression leaving him.

'God, I'm tired.' He rubbed one hand along his jaw and Yvie heard the rasp of his beard that would soon need shaving. His eyes rose to meet hers. 'So we haven't met before today,' he said flatly. 'So be it. We'll leave it at that.' He turned towards the door pausing with his hand on the knob, turning his head so that he was looking back at her. 'For the moment,' he added quietly before he stepped out of the flat and was gone.

Next morning Yvie sat at her desk and gazed tiredly at the pile of work in front of her. The very last thing she felt like doing was working. Her head felt tight and her eyes were heavy and gritty.

She picked up a couple of memos from the pile and read the first paragraph of the top one before she realised she wasn't even taking in the message. She sighed and threw them down again, her fingers sliding beneath her hair to massage the tight muscles in the back of her neck.

This wasn't getting her very far. She retrieved the memos. If she immersed herself in her work it would take her mind off other things, other problems. Like Josh Graham and their conversation of the evening before, for instance.

She was in a turmoil over that, tossing and turning in her bed and even allowing it to cloud her concentration this morning driving to work. She'd very nearly missed her exit as his words replayed themselves over and over in her mind, torturing her in a way she had thought impossible after all this time.

By all accounts he had been searching for her. But why? Why would he be seeking her out. Unless he ... No! If he still harboured some attraction towards her then that was his own lookout. There was no point in going into it all again. It was over. She'd spent agonising days, weeks, months turning the whole sordid affair over in her mind and she wasn't going to permit herself to start again. It was in the past.

If she'd allowed him to kiss her last night then there was always the chance that somewhere deep inside her an ember may have continued to glow, waiting to flare at the touch of his lips. No way! she admonished herself forcefully. Not one spark remained, she had made painfully sure of that. It was an impossible thought. But ... she wasn't going to put it to the test. It was over. She'd leave it at that.

So she had to work with him. Well, she would. She was an adult, wasn't she? So she'd manage somehow.

The door opened and Abby stuck her head inside Yvie's office.

'Morning, Yvie,' she greeted the other girl brightly making Yvie feel even more tired. 'How are you?'

'Fine,' replied Yvie, thinking nothing could be further from the truth.

Abby came inside and perched on the edge of Yvie's desk. 'Well?' she asked, flicking her long dark hair back over her shoulder.

'Well what?' As if Yvie didn't know 'well what?'.

'Oh, Yvie! Josh Graham, that's what. What's he like? As gorgeous as his photo?' Abby grinned, her dark eyes flashing.

Yvie shrugged. 'I guess the old saying applies, beauty is in the eye etc. Or maybe, one man's meat.'

'Everyone's right,' said Abby, shaking her head. 'You are unflappable. Imagine meeting Josh Graham and not even batting an eyelid. I would have been, well, incoherent at least.'

'No, you wouldn't.' Yvie smiled at the other girl. 'You would have been your usual charming self, I've no doubt about that.'

'And I'm not so sure.' Abby sighed. 'He really is attractive, you have to admit that, Yvie.'

'Oh, he's not bad looking but blonds are notorious for being untrustworthy, aren't they?' she quipped. If you only knew, Abby, just how untrustworthy this one was, Yvie mused to herself.

'In my experience, hair colour has nothing to do with it. You get them bad and you get them good. Anyway,' Abby stood up, 'all this is a bit pointless I suppose, Josh Graham being married and all. What's she like, the lucky lady? Mousey and unremarkable or absolutely gorgeous?'

'I don't really know,' Yvie got out. 'She wasn't travelling with them. He only had his son with him.'

'The woman must be mad letting a guy like Josh Graham out of her sight. I'd be clinging like the proverbial vine.' Abby crossed to the door. 'Takes all types I guess. She must trust him completely. Oh!' she paused and grimaced. 'I almost forgot what I came for. Dan wants to see you in his office. I left him grinning from ear to ear. There is one happy publisher. See you later.'

'Bye,' Yvie said absently.

Funny, she hadn't given Josh's wife a thought last night. That same ache clutched inside her. Four years on and she still didn't even know what Renee Graham even looked like. All she knew was that he had belonged to another woman, a woman who bore his name, had given him a son. And who had every reason in the world to expect his faithfulness. At the time Josh had tried to tell her that the marriage was not a success but all she'd understood was the fact that he wasn't free to love her, to make love to her.

Yvie groaned inwardly. There was no way she was going to cope with the next few months if she didn't stop rehashing it every moment. Resolutely she stood up and squared her shoulders. If she didn't go into Dan he'd begin to wonder where she was. And she knew what, or rather who, he'd want to discuss. Well, she'd simply have to face it. It would be just another hurdle.

Opening her door she started down the corridor towards Dan's office only to run into a solid body hurrying out of another office to the left.

'Hey, Yvie, great running into you.' Paul Rosetti smiled down at her, his dark eyes mischievous in his very handsome face. He was tall and dark haired and managed to be very nice even though women flocked to him in droves.

He kept his arms around Yvie holding her lightly against him. 'If I'd known all it would take was an accidental collision to get you this close I'd have machinated it sooner,' he grinned and Yvie smiled back stepping away from him.

'Unhand me before I get trampled by the Paul Rosetti Fan Club,' she laughed easily. Since their first meeting when Paul had made a concerted play for her and Yvie had gently but firmly declined they had been the best of friends.

'There's not a spark of adventure in you, Yvie Dean,' he touched the tip of her nose with his finger. 'You going in to see Dan?'

Yvie nodded.

'No need to ask who'll be the topic of conversation. The whole office has been twittering about it all morning. How did it go at the airport last night anyway?'

'Fine.' Yvie replied casually.

Paul raised his eyebrows and shook his head in disbelief. 'She just meets the great Josh Graham and all she can say is fine.' Paul picked up her wrist and made an exaggerated show of taking

Yvie's pulse. 'Just checking to see if your heart's still beating.'

'He seemed quite nice,' Yvie said as normally as she could.

'Quite nice.' Paul mimicked Yvie's accent. 'You think he's quite nice while Abby runs around checking her makeup every minute or so just on the off chance that Josh Graham calls in at the office. And as for Lori and Chrissie,' he mentioned the two typists, 'well, we won't be getting much out of them until the man himself has been and gone.'

'I doubt he'll be coming into the office,' Yvie said as evenly as she could manage. 'After all, he's here to finish his book. I expect he'll be closeting himself away once he gets over his jet lag.'

Paul put his finger conspiratorially to his lips. 'Don't let them hear that, we could have a mutiny on our hands. They're living in hope,' he grinned.

'Now don't tell me they'd notice any other man when you flash those brown eyes at them because I don't believe it,' Yvie teased lightly.

Paul laughed. 'You are magnificent for my ego, Yvie darling. I don't know why I don't marry you and be done with it. Can't you see us making our own little nest, heart of mine.'

'Not quite,' she laughed with him, feeling decidedly better as she turned to tap on Dan's door.

'Morning, Yvie.' Dan beamed at her, obviously in the best of spirits. 'Well, everything go off okay?'

Yvie shrugged. 'Yes, I guess so.'

Dan's brow clouded. 'What's the matter? Didn't he like the house?'

'Of course he liked the house and nothing's the matter,' Yvie hastened to reassure her boss, feeling a little guilty because of her lack of response.

'You got them settled in all right?' Dan persisted.

'Mmm. I, uh, we stopped at Vista Point to look at the bridge and the lights and then I took them straight home. It was a long flight so I'm sure they just wanted to get to bed.' Yvie swallowed nervously, telling herself to forget her run-in with Josh the evening before.

'You're right there,' Dan nodded. 'Better tell him not to worry about calling me until he's over the flight. Anyway, he can send any messages with you,' he finished grandly.

'Oh, Dan, now look, I probably won't even see that much of them,' Yvie appealed to him. 'I mean, he'll be working on his book and I'll be away from the house all day. I think it might be best if he kept in touch with you by telephone. It's more direct and there's no chance of any distortion of the facts.'

'Distortion of the facts!' Dan laughed heartily. 'I somehow can't see you distorting anything, young lady. If I didn't know better I'd say you had a more personal reason for wanting to keep out of Josh Graham's way.'

Yvie swallowed. 'What . . . what do you mean?'

'He's a nice looking guy, wouldn't you say?'

'I suppose so.' Yvie flushed.

'And you're a nice looking young woman.' Dan grinned. 'Haven't I always said that? Why, if I was twenty years younger and didn't feel so paternal towards you I'd give Josh Graham a run for his money but,' he raised his hands and let them fall, 'that's how it goes.'

'Dan, for heaven's sake, I'm not interested in Josh Graham any more than he's interested in me.' Somewhere inside Yvie jeered at herself.

'Now don't get your feathers ruffled. I was only teasing you. Besides, you know I've always fancied myself as a bit of a matchmaker.' Dan winked and Yvie had to smile.

'Well, don't pull that stunt with me. Okay?'

'Okay.' Dan agreed and then sobered. 'But he is happy with the house and everything, isn't he, because if he isn't we'll have to find him somewhere else.'

Yvie wanted to say that Josh Graham wasn't a god nor was he the only big name author on their books but instead she merely reassured Dan and then left him happily contemplating Josh's new novel.

And that Josh must have been working on his manuscript was apparent as the rest of the week flew past, for Yvie saw neither hide nor hair of Josh or Tim and she began to wonder if perhaps she had built the whole affair into a greater problem than it appeared it was going to be. It seemed she would be seeing very little of Josh, a fact about which she was well pleased. And it also meant she had little to report to Dan thus ensuring that he contacted Josh himself via the telephone.

On Saturday morning Yvie braved the garage through necessity and hurried through her weekly washing. There wasn't a sound from the house overhead although Yvie was tensed for the slightest movement from above.

After lunch, dressed in faded jeans, sneakers and a loose outsized T-shirt, Yvie tackled cleaning out her small fish tank. She'd been promising her three goldfish that she would attend to them for a couple of weeks and she set to with vigour. Soon all was to rights and she stood back to admire her handiwork.

A soft tap on the door through to the garage caused Yvie to jump. She froze, waiting. The knock was repeated, a little louder this time.

She knew she'd have to answer it. She could hardly pretend she wasn't home when her radio was beating out a popular tune. Switching it off Yvie reluctantly crossed to the door, reaching out her hand to slowly open it.

'Hi!' Tim Graham stood in the doorway, his hands shoved into the back pockets of his jeans.

'Hello.' Yvie smiled faintly, relieved and yet disappointed that it wasn't his father who stood there.

'I saw the, uh, the table tennis table over there by the wall,' Tim pointed to the other side of the garage, 'and I wondered if you could give me permission to use it, or maybe ask Mr Kirkoff if I could. Dad said I had to ask first.'

'I'm sure it would be all right with Dan for you to use it.' Yvie's smile widened now that she could relax. 'In fact, I used to play on it myself. I just let down one side and played against the other side.'

'You play table tennis?' Tim arched his brows in surprise over eyes the same shade as his father's.

'Yes. Why the surprise? Think I'm past any form of energetic movement?'

Tim grinned. 'No, I didn't say that. I don't think you're that old. Really.'

'Thank you,' Yvie said exaggeratedly. 'We'll have to have a game some time, won't we?'

'How about now?' Tim pressed eagerly.

'Oh, well, I was——' She stopped as the bright eagerness faded from Tim's face, leaving that same expression of bored sulkiness.

'I guess you're busy,' he said flatly.

'I was, but then again it's Saturday so I suppose my housework will wait until later.' She smiled at him.

'Great. There's a couple of bats and some balls with the table.' He looked a little sheepish. 'I, uh, I saw them there before.'

Yvie followed him across the garage.

'Shall I get Dad to help us lift the table out?' he asked.

'No. I think you and I will be able to manage it,' Yvie replied quickly. 'It looks heavier than it is.'

One on each side of the table they half lifted half slid it out from the wall and Yvie lowered both halves into playing position. She wiped off the dust with a rag.

'There we are. The net should be here somewhere.'

'Here it is.' Tim began attaching the net on to one side of the table and he held it steady while Yvie did the other side.

'Thanks for having a game with me, Yvie. To tell you the truth I was beginning to get a bit sick of my own company,' he shrugged, 'what with Dad working so hard on his book and all.'

'I haven't seen you about since the night you arrived. What have you been up to?' Yvie asked him casually.

'Nothing much,' he replied. 'Studying a bit.'

'I suppose you're doing correspondence lessons while you're here, are you?'

'Mmm,' Tim nodded, 'and I have to catch up on a fair bit of stuff. I, uh, I missed some school so Dad thought it would be a good opportunity to get myself up to date.' He grimaced. 'But he doesn't have to do it. It's dead boring. Except maybe history. I don't mind that. I like reading about it but,' he shrugged again.

'It's a different thing when you have to study it,' Yvie finished for him and he nodded.

'I was just getting into wargaming before we left. I read a couple of books from the library on it. Have you heard of it?'

Yvie nodded. 'It's setting up history battles with toy soldiers, isn't it?'

'Sort of. You have to be really authentic though. Dad bought me a big set of toy soldiers when we were in Australia and I'm going to build up a collection.' Tim paused. 'You're Australian, aren't you?'

'Yes. I've been working here for two years now.'

'I guess you've done lots of sightseeing.'

'I did when I first arrived here. I was pretty excited about it all in the beginning but I'm a little more blasé about it now,' she grinned.

'Dad says as soon as I catch up on my schoolwork I can take some tours. I'd love to go out to Yosemite National Park. Have you been there, Yvie?'

'Yes. I spent two weeks out there last year with some friends. We did some hiking and some cycling. It's a beautiful place.'

Tim sighed. 'I've seen some brochures on the park and it looks fantastic. I sure hope Dad will have time to take me out there before we go home. Wish I didn't have all that extra work to do.'

'How come you missed school?' Yvie asked him as he handed her her pingpong bat. 'Were you sick?'

'No, not exactly.' Tim looked away, his eyes sliding from hers. 'Do you want to serve first?' he asked quickly, effectively changing the subject.

They played well together and were evenly matched. Time passed and before they knew it the sun was setting and they had to switch on the garage lights so that they could continue their game.

'Next point for the match,' Tim reminded Yvie as he prepared to serve.

The ball flew back and forth until Tim outmanoeuvred Yvie. She made a desperate lunge, her sneaker clad foot slipping, and she miss-hit the ball as she fell in an unceremonious heap on the table top.

'Hey, Yvie, are you okay?' Tim asked with concern.

As Yvie went to push herself upright strong hands clasped her waist, lifting her, turning her around so that their bodies met thigh to thigh.

CHAPTER FOUR

'ARE you all right?' Josh's words echoed his son's.

'Yes, of course,' Yvie got out breathlessly. She could feel herself beginning to quiver inside as his nearness brought her senses screaming to the surface.

Slowly Josh let her slide downwards until her feet touched the floor and for what seemed like an eternity they stood there, touching, tension rising. With a will of its own Yvie's body moulded itself to the hard contours of Josh's in a rush of bittersweet recall. Time stood still and then spun backwards, tripping over itself until they were back four years, locked together on a moonlit beach, lost in each other.

'We've just had a fantastic game, Dad.'

Tim's words began to sluggishly filter through the sensual euphoria that had insinuated itself between Yvie and her firm resolutions and the sound of Tim's voice reminded her of those intentions.

Don't let Josh Graham too close. But he was close. And it was such exquisite pleasure to stand again in the circle of his arms, feel the hard strength beneath her hands where they rested against his cotton shirt. Don't let Josh Graham too close.

Yvie tried valiantly to draw herself together. She was allowing herself to be manoeuvred into the very position she had assured herself she would avoid at all cost. Her body stiffened, her hands pushing against the wall of his chest. For a split second she thought he was going to use his superior strength to hold her fast for she felt his own muscles flex, but very slowly he relaxed, releasing her and she stepped shakily away from him. And she felt suddenly quite cold.

'Yvie's not a bad player.' Tim walked around the table to stand beside his father. 'In fact she almost beat me.' He grinned happily as he spun the bat between his fingers.

'Did she?' Josh turned his gaze from his son to Yvie. 'Where did you learn to play?' he asked her easily although his eyes roaming over her body spoke a language that held a totally different meaning.

'Larry, my husband, taught me,' she replied throatily. 'He's something of an expert at table tennis.'

The smile faded from Josh's face and his eyes lost their warmth as his expression hardened, his lips thinning.

'I learnt to play at school,' Tim informed Yvie, not sensing the undercurrents that swelled between the two adults. 'We played a lot in our lunch breaks and even arranged tournaments.' Tim leant back against the table. 'Hey, maybe your husband will give me a game. When will he be home?'

Josh's eyes swept Yvie's face with cold inflexibility and he couldn't have helped but notice the dull flush that suffused her cheeks. His eyes narrowed and Yvie swallowed agitatedly.

'I'm not sure. But he probably won't get leave before you return home,' she improvised quickly experiencing a rush of immediate guilt at her falsehood that wasn't strictly an untruth. Larry was at sea as far as she knew and not due for leave and it was months since she'd heard from him.

'Oh! Pity.' Tim shrugged and tapped his bat on his jean-clad leg. 'Shall we have another game? I'll give you a chance to get even.'

Yvie glanced at her wristwatch. 'Well, it's getting rather late,' she began.

'And it's almost dinnertime,' Josh finished. 'What say we eat out?'

'Hey, great idea, Dad,' Tim agreed enthusiastically. 'I was getting a bit sick of our cooking anyway. Where shall we go?'

'I thought we'd leave that up to Yvie as she'll be more familiar with the local restaurants.' Josh turned back to her.

'Oh, I don't think I, well,' she stammered.

'We'd love to have you join us, if you have nothing else on, that is.' Josh's tone seemed to challenge her.

How Yvie wished she could honestly tell him she had made other plans for the evening but it was suddenly beyond her to prevaricate. And all at once the night ahead gaped before her lonely as a shadowy chasm.

'No, I haven't anything else planned,' she replied evenly. It wasn't as though she was going to be alone with Josh. Tim would be there.

'Do you know of any good places to eat?' Tim's eyes shone, his expression striking a chord from the past. He was so very much like Josh in some

ways, that totally alive expression, the way he
held his head.

Yvie felt a wave of ineffable feeling for the boy
wash over her, a sensation all mixed up with Josh
and the past. Yes, remember the past, she
reminded herself severely and the bitterness
began to rise again.

He could have been your child, jeered a
persistent voice inside her. He could have been
your son, this boy, almost a young man, who was
so much like his father. Pain rose to almost choke
her. Tim wasn't her son. Her child ... Yvie
stopped her thoughts with sudden mercilessness.

How could she have been so weak as to allow
herself to be talked into sharing a meal with Josh
Graham. She must be mad. Or a total masochist,
she chastised herself.

'Yes,' she heard herself reply. 'There's a nice
restaurant not far from here. Dan and I have
dined there occasionally. I could ... perhaps I
could give them a ring to see if they have a table.'

'Fine.' Josh consulted his own watch. 'For, say,
an hour's time?' He raised one eyebrow enquiringly. 'That should give us time to get ready,
shouldn't it?'

'All right.' Yvie walked towards her flat and
felt Josh and Tim following her.

In her agitation she fumbled with the telephone
directory and it slipped to the floor. She reached
to retrieve it as a strong brown hand did the
same. Their fingers touched, ignited that flame of
awareness, so that Yvie drew her hand away as
though she'd been burned and her heartbeats
raced in response to his touch.

Josh straightened, passing her the telephone book, and Yvie took it from him, unable to meet his gaze. She flipped jerkily through the pages taking ages to find the number of the restaurant.

Yes, they had a table for three in one hour. Yvie replaced the receiver.

'Great!' beamed Tim.

'We'll be down as soon as we're ready,' Josh said turning Tim in the direction of the door and giving him a little shove.

Yvie stood and stared at the closed door after they'd gone. Why couldn't the restaurant have been booked out? After all, it was quite popular. Why had she agreed to go with them? Well, you did, she told herself exasperatedly, so now you'll have to carry it through.

She took a quick shower and wrapped herself in her towelling robe. Now what was she going to wear? Yvie flicked through the dresses hanging in her wardrobe, settling on a particular favourite. She always felt good in this dress and she was going to need all the moral support the dress could give her.

Taking off her robe she slipped the soft aqua coloured dress over her head. The neckline was elasticised and she pulled it down so that the tops of her shoulders were bare. A four inch frill trimmed with matching aqua lace came away from the neckline and sat over her arms. The waist was gathered emphasising her firm breasts and the skirt fell in soft folds over her hips. Yvie donned a pair of delicate, white, high heeled sandals and returned to her mirror to lightly dust her face with makeup.

She used a pale aqua eyeshadow and darkened her long lashes with mascara. Her face looked a trifle pale so she touched her cheekbones with blush before applying her lipstick with a far from steady hand. Her fair hair fell to her shoulders in soft curling waves and in the glow from the artificial light it shimmered silkily as she moved.

Well, she was ready, as ready as she'd ever be. She paused to gaze critically at her reflection. She had changed so much for she was hardly the naïve teenager she'd been when she first met Josh Graham.

The weight she'd lost had thinned her face emphasising her good bone structure and her hair was longer and worn in a far more sophisticated style. All that was simply physical. Superficial.

Emotionally the change had been far greater. Four years ago she had been full of life, and very sure of her love, a young woman so far apart from the Yvie Dean of today that she might have been a totally different person. That Yvie Dean, Yvie Matthews as she'd been then, had been so blindly trusting, ingenuous, that Yvie could almost find her ludicrous. Yvie Matthews would have run, in her innocence, straight into Josh Graham's arms without even stopping to consider any possibility of rejection so sure of her love had she been. And so sure that her love was irrefutably reciprocated.

After their first meeting a week had passed before they'd seen Josh again. Yvie had spent that week in a fever of alternating excitement and despair. It seemed that the handsome Josh Graham had become imprinted on her mind overriding and totally overshadowing her thoughts.

She daydreamed, planning all sorts of conversations with him, what she'd say when she saw him again. And she was convinced she would be seeing him again. His eyes had held that promise in their blue depths as he'd taken his leave of them.

When he did return on the following weekend all the scintillating things she'd been going to say to him simply escaped her and she'd stood there tonguetied just managing to smile at him. They'd talked together, Yvie, her father and Josh, and they'd walked along the beach for a short way. Josh had pointed out the unit he was going to be using.

The picture of the warm whitish sand, the surging turquoise sea and the clear blue skies was as vivid in Yvie's mind's eye as it had been four years ago. It was a backdrop that seemed only fitting for someone as tall, as tanned, as potently attractive as Josh Graham had been to Yvie that day. And every day after.

His dark denim shorts had hugged his tanned muscular thighs and the sun had bleached to white the fine hair on his legs. His light, short-sleeved knit shirt only accentuated the breadth of his shoulders, the developed biceps in his upper arms. He was so completely fit and vital that he took Yvie's breath away. She had never met a man who affected her quite like Josh Graham did.

It was amazing how easily, how intensely, the sensations of that sunlit afternoon came back to her now, so clear in each minute detail. First and foremost was her joy at being near him, of being able to look at him. At the strand of fair hair that the breeze blew across Josh's brow, the way his eyes crinkled up against the glare of the sun on sand and sea. And his smile as he turned to her.

It was all so very real. As though it had happened only yesterday. She could see again the upward tilt of the corners of his mouth, the way his eyes danced when he laughed at something her father said. And the expression in those eyes when his gaze fell on her, moving over her long legs, tanned too from her surfing and sunbathing, rising over her rounded hips and full young breasts, making her quiver inside. And how his eyes lingered on her lips until they began to tingle, as though he'd physically touched his mouth to hers.

Yvie shivered slightly as those memories escaped from the shadows of the darkest corner of her mind to which she'd banished them. Yes, it was all so real. She could almost hear Josh's deep voice as he told them he was moving into his unit on Wednesday. And before Yvie could stop herself she'd hesitantly asked him to dinner. After all, she'd added quickly, he would be driving up from Brisbane, settling in, and he wouldn't feel like cooking himself a meal. Her father had agreed, adding his voice to the invitation.

And Josh had accepted. Their eyes met. Held. And the message had been so clear to Yvie. She couldn't mistake the fact that he was as attracted to her as she was attracted to him.

Wednesday had seemed an eternity in coming. Yvie took great pains over the meal and was in a fever of agitation that something would go wrong. But it hadn't. It had all been perfect.

They'd sat around the table, Josh and her father talking shop and Yvie content to listen, her heart swelling each time Josh paused to draw her into the conversation. After the meal the men had insisted on dealing with the dishes and with that done they'd retired to the twilight-lit patio for coffee.

Josh then suggested a walk along the beach but Jim Matthews had declined.

'Yvie will go with you,' he said, 'she's the beachcomber of the family.'

'But Dad,' Yvie protested, suddenly embarrassed, 'I can't leave you here alone.'

'Rubbish,' Jim admonished her. 'I'll be fine. Besides, there's a show on television I particularly wanted to see. Now, off you go, and enjoy the walk.'

And so they'd gone, just the two of them, kicking off their shoes and walking side by side along the moonlit beach. It seemed ages to Yvie before Josh broke the silence between them.

'Your father appears to be improving,' he remarked.

'Yes, he is. His doctors are quite pleased with his progress I think,' she replied a little breathlessly, 'although he still seems to get tired so easily. He desperately wants to get back to work, but he's not ready for that yet.'

'I can tell he misses it all.' Josh paused. 'I have a feeling I shall as well. For a while at least,' he added reflectively.

'Have you made a start on your book yet?' she asked him shyly.

'Not exactly. I've jotted down plenty of notes and a very rough outline. I did that ages ago, preparing for the day I'd finally make the break.'

'And now you've done it,' Yvie finished.

'Now I've done it,' he repeated. 'For better or worse,' he added wryly.

'What will it be about?' The question came out and then she realised he may not want to talk about it.

But he did, hesitantly at first, and then Yvie was caught up in his enthusiasm. That night she'd known Josh's book would be successful, it couldn't help but be. He brought it alive for her.

'The only part I'm undecided about is the ending. Should the hero get the heroine or should some quirk of fate keep them apart?'

'Well, I'm a sucker for a happy ending,' Yvie told him. 'There's a lot to be said for the hero and the heroine walking off hand in hand into the sunset.'

Yvie realised then that they had stopped walking, and were standing facing each other, less than an arm's length apart. She felt drawn to him, had to fight a rising impulse to move that short distance forward that would bring her up against him. She felt hot all over, and then cold, and she swallowed nervously.

'I suppose everyone likes a happy ending.' She tried to laugh brightly but the sound was stilted to her ears for he was looking at her, she could see that in the bright moonlight.

'So you like happy endings?' Josh asked softly.

Yvie's vocal chords seemed momentarily paralysed and she couldn't form an answer. They stood looking at each other, not moving, held in the rising tension of that portentous moment.

A soft shallow wave swirled about their feet, cool against Yvie's hot legs, and she laughed a little self-consciously, moving out of reach of the water, away from Josh. He followed her and his hand reached out, his fingers twining with hers with a naturalness that to Yvie felt so right.

'Oh, Yvie,' she heard him breathe softly, his words almost drowned by the sound of the sea. 'Do you know just how beautiful you are?'

He stepped closer, his hands now reaching out to rest on her waist, burning through the thin cotton of her dress.

'Josh, please.' Yvie's voice caught in her throat, although she couldn't have told whether her appeal was to be released or to be drawn closer.

'I haven't been able to get you out of my mind since I met you. You've haunted me day and night.'

He was so much closer. His legs were touching hers with only the thin materials of his slacks and her dress separating them and to Yvie it was very nearly no barrier at all. In her heightened awareness she could feel every hard contour of his body setting her ablaze and when his head lowered towards hers she raised her mouth to meet his.

His lips were cool and moved slowly, lightly against hers, nibbling gently until she relaxed completely, unconsciously against him, her own lips opening inviting the gradual deepening of his kisses. All her inhibitions vanished beneath Josh's all consuming desire, desire she matched with her own. His kisses sparked a flame inside her that ignited in a thunderous roar in her ears as it rose to engulf her.

She was straining against him now, her body craving an intimacy that was impossible on a public beach. Although, had Josh laid her down on the warm sand and made love to her, she doubted she could have resisted him. It was always that way between them.

Yvie had never known herself capable of such a response to a man's kisses. She'd been kissed before but she'd always been in total command of the situation. Never had she been so lost to herself.

Josh released her lips and they both fought for breath.

'My God, Yvie,' he murmured roughly, his voice rumbling from deep in his chest. 'I knew it would be like this with us.'

He clasped her to him, his hands playing down the length of her spine, his lips teasingly seeking her earlobe sending shivers of desire coursing through her. Then his lips slid downwards to the curve of her throat lingering there before sliding over her bare shoulder.

His mouth found hers again and his hand moved from her back around to find the fullness of her breast where it strained against the hardness of his chest. His fingers had no trouble locating the hard peak of her nipple and she moaned raggedly as he carressed her.

'Yvie. Yvie, what you do to me,' he sighed brokenly as he moved against her, leaving her in no doubt that he was as aroused as she was.

And Yvie luxuriated in it, in the way he could lift her to such heights with a mere caress, in the way she could arouse him.

His hand left her breast and went to her shoulder as he reluctantly put her away from him.

'Josh?' Yvie whispered his name brokenly. 'What's the matter?'

'Nothing,' he replied softly, running one finger gently along the line of her jaw. 'Except that what we're doing is far too private to continue here. And perhaps that's for the best, best that I remembered that anyway,' he added ruefully.

'What do you mean?' Yvie wanted so much for him to put his arms around her again, to feel his heart thudding beneath the palms of her hands.

Josh gave a short low laugh. 'I mean that you have this earth-shattering effect on me.' His voice dropped caressingly. 'I almost lost my head a moment ago.'

'I . . . I did too,' Yvie admitted, her eyes falling as she ran her hand nervously through her short fair hair.

Josh lifted her chin with gentle fingers. 'Did I frighten you, Yvie?' he asked and she shook her head.

'No. I guess I frightened myself,' she swallowed self-consciously. 'I've never, well, felt this way before.' Her eyes took in the hard masculine planes of his face, muted by the moonlight, and she knew she was in love with him.

Josh's arms reached around her, binding her to him and they stood there locked together, not needing words, Josh's cheek resting against her hair. Yvie exalted in the sensations of his muscular body in her arms, of her hands playing over the strength of his back, and the feel of each breath he took.

'I could stay like this all night but,' Josh sighed and leaned back from her, his eyes finishing his sentence. He lowered his head and placed a feathersoft kiss on the tip of her nose. 'Your father will be beginning to wonder where we are. Let's go back.'

And hand in hand, wrapped in their discovery of each other, they had strolled back along the beach to the house, rejoining Yvie's father.

This flat in California had seemed remote enough from that beach in south eastern Queensland, far enough away for Yvie to forget. Until now it had been. But now it wasn't far enough away and she hadn't forgotten.

Yvie squeezed her eyes tightly closed and gripped the top of her dressing table. Those echoes from the past had caught up with her with painful ease, laying bare the wound she had thought safely healed. All it had taken to bring it back was the advent of Josh Graham. He'd brought it screaming back.

Why was she suffering this agony all over again? The pain was as real as it had been way back then. If you didn't care it wouldn't hurt. The thought sprang into her mind but she rejected it just as quickly. Of course she didn't still care. All that was over. Josh had killed her love as surely as she was standing here. He'd seen her, wanted her, taken and then discarded her. She couldn't possibly still care about a man who had treated her so callously.

In her mirror Yvie's eyes reflected her misery. And she was about to go out to dinner with him. She must be mad! Stark raving mad! She straightened and relaxed her grip on the dressing table top, flexing her stiffened fingers. She just wouldn't go. It was as simple as that. She was walking purposefully towards the door to the garage when a knock sounded on it.

'Hi, Yvie! Are you ready?' Tim stood smiling at her, his face aglow, so obviously excited about their outing. He had changed into a pair of slacks, a shirt and sweater and had taken time to brush his unruly curls into some order.

How could she tell him she had changed her mind? Yvie experienced a rush of guilt.

'I like your dress. It looks nice.' Tim complimented Yvie and then flushed in embarrassment.

Yvie smiled at him. 'Thank you. You don't look bad yourself.'

Tim laughed then and they were still chuckling when Josh came down the stairs and walked towards them. His glance went from his son to Yvie as he approached them, his eyes slowly taking in her now completely still form, lighting on the length of her bare legs, her dress, her face, and Yvie felt as though he'd touched her. Her body began to come alive and she was powerless to stop it. She longed to reach out, feel the firmness of his flesh beneath her fingers.

'What's the joke?' Josh asked, smiling at them.

Yvie's breath caught in her chest. That smile . . .

'Oh, nothing, Dad,' Tim grinned. 'Yvie and I were just flattering each other.'

Josh raised an eyebrow at his son.

'I said Yvie looked great and she said I did, too,' Tim chuckled again, highly amused.

Josh's glance returned to Yvie. 'I can't dispute that,' he said softly, his eyes darkening as they settled on her lips.

'I'll collect my bag and jacket,' she said quickly and turned back into her flat.

So it seemed she was committed to going along with Josh and Tim tonight. So much for keeping everything cool and distant. Yvie almost laughed at that thought. When it came to Josh Graham she would have to be a fool to deny that she found him anything but unsettling.

The drive further up the hill to the restaurant took a matter of minutes and after babying her car up the last precipitous gradient Yvie was thankful to hand her keys to the parking attendant before she led them up a steep flight of steps into the restaurant's lobby.

Their table was by the plate glass windows and once they were seated the waiter passed them their menus with a flourish.

'Wow! What a view!' Tim remarked enthusiastically. 'This is even more spectacular than back at the house.'

The panorama displayed the city dressed in blinking nightlights, the ribbons of headlights on the Bay and Golden Gate Bridges and the intermittent flashes of boat lights on the bay. Their vantage point being higher the scene was more widespread than the view from the house and it was the focus of attention of most of the diners in the tastefully decorated little restaurant.

'I'm glad I brought my camera.' Tim gazed about him. 'I'll go out on the deck later and take a couple of time exposure shots. It should come out great.'

'It is beautiful, isn't it?' Yvie smiled at him. 'And in two years I can still marvel at it.'

She turned her smiling gaze on Josh to see if he was enjoying the view. But he was watching her and the subdued light of the dining room only intensified the blatant message in their inky blue depths.

Looking quickly away Yvie gave her menu her concentrated attention but the names of the delectable dishes written on the page in front of her were running together in an unintelligible blur. For heaven's sake, Yvie chastised herself angrily, this was going to have to stop.

How could she allow one look from Josh Graham to disorientate her the way it had? She was beginning to think she must be feeble-minded. But the naked awareness in Josh's eyes had stirred an answering arousal in herself with an incontrovertible ease. As easy as it had always been, she would admit if she was at all honest with herself.

'I think I'll have the steak,' Tim said with anticipation and Josh decided on the same, with a shrimp cocktail as an entrée.

Yvie chose salmon although she had a feeling she was going to be hard pressed making a show of eating it with Josh so close. If she moved her leg just a fraction she knew it would come into contact with his leg and the thought was disconcerting, and yet exhilarating.

Tim happily carried the conversation until Josh's cocktail arrived and as he forked the succulent seafood flesh into his mouth Yvie couldn't prevent herself from watching him surreptitiously through her lashes. She couldn't help herself. Her eyes seemed to devour him, the strong hand raising the food to his lips and his lips . . . Yvie swallowed convulsively.

'Want to try some?' Josh asked softly as his eyes met hers, caught her watching him, and held her gaze.

'Oh, no. No, thanks. I'll wait for the main course,' she hastened to assure him.

'It's exceptionally good. Here. Open up.' He carried the fork across to her and Yvie automatically opened her mouth. He put the seafood morsel against her lips and Yvie took the mouthful.

He'd done such a thing a number of times before in the past, let her taste from the food on his plate, shared a piece of fruit with her, but never before had his attentive actions affected her quite so devastatingly. Yvie's body burned with her heightened awareness of him watching as she chewed the piece of shrimp and the taste of the food completely escaped her. Josh had transformed a simple deed into a sensual gesture and he was as aware of the fact as she was.

His thigh brushed hers and his touch flamed that fire glowing in the pit of her stomach. Yvie clenched her hands together in her lap. My God, he had as potent a hold on her as he'd ever had and she had to draw a halt to it.

Deliberately Yvie moved her leg away from

his, but the familiar ache of need remained. How her body craved his, yearned for the long remembered touch of his hands, his tongue, finding secret places only he could locate. The tension soared between them, thick and taut and their eyes held.

'Yuck! I don't know how you can eat that stuff.' Tim's voice broke the enmeshing spell.

Yvie dragged her eyes from Josh and turned with relief to Tim.

'It's dreadful,' Tim screwed up his nose. 'Poor little shrimps.'

'Don't you like seafood?' she asked him breathily.

'I don't mind some fish but I don't like crabs and prawns and things like that. I'd much rather beef or chicken.' He turned to his father. 'We had some great barbeques when we lived in Australia, didn't we, Dad?'

Josh paused, his fork hovering over his dish. He shot a quick glance at Yvie before replying. 'Yes, we did.'

'What part of Australia do you come from Yvie?' Tim asked innocently.

'Brisbane,' she replied softly.

'Hey, we lived just outside Brisbane while Dad was working for a newspaper there. It was a great house with a swimming pool and a half court tennis court. I really liked it.' He sobered. 'But Mum and Gran thought it was too hot in Brisbane.' Tim played absently with his cutlery, his young face sad.

Pain clutched at Yvie. So those regular trips down to Brisbane had not been to do research for his book as Yvie had imagined they were, as he'd allowed her to think they were. His wife had been in Brisbane all the time. He'd never told her that and somehow she had afterwards assumed that his family had been in England. Not that it mattered, Yvie told herself cynically. The fact that he had a wife at all had been the only important thing.

With these reflections churning around inside her Yvie found making conversation more than a little difficult. Josh also, whatever his own thoughts, seemed loath to make small talk and so it was Tim who did most of the talking. Once he started entertaining Yvie with tales of the differences between school in England and school in Australia time passed quickly. Yvie even found herself relaxing enough to laugh at Tim's anecdotes. She was amazed that this could be the same sulky boy who arrived at the airport less than a week ago.

Tim's conversation carried them through the main course and they all declined the dessert. Yvie and Josh ordered coffee.

'I'll go out and try for some shots while you're drinking your coffee.' Tim stood up, taking his camera from the table. 'I won't be long.'

He walked out through the door on to the deck and Yvie watched him go with rising disquiet. She was alone again with Josh. Her fingers nervously found her coffee cup and she raised it unsteadily to her lips, keeping her gaze averted from Josh.

'Tim's pretty keen with his camera,' she remarked at last when she could bear the brooding silence no longer.

'Mmm.' Josh appeared to draw himself slowly from his thoughts, far from pleasant ones if his frown was any indication. 'He's not a bad photographer. He's taken some exceptionally good shots lately.'

There was silence again and Yvie searched agitatedly for an innocuous subject to discuss. 'How . . .' she swallowed restively. 'How's your book coming along?' She managed to keep her voice steady, matter-of-fact.

'Fine,' he replied drily and Yvie looked up sharply at his tone.

Josh's lips had tightened. 'Did Dan ask you to check that out?'

'No, of course not,' Yvie told him firmly. 'Dan wouldn't do that. If he wanted to know he'd ask you himself, believe me. That's not Dan's style.'

'I guess you're right.' Josh sighed, his eyes on the dark liquid in his coffee cup. 'I'm sorry. I suppose I'm a little touchy these days.'

'Why should you be? Dan hasn't pressured you, has he? I couldn't imagine him pushing anyone.' Let alone someone as forceful and self-possessed as the Josh Graham she had known, Yvie added to herself.

'No, he hasn't pressured me.' Josh shrugged. 'As you say, that's not his style. I suppose it all comes back to me. I've had trouble concentrating on this book, what with one thing and another.' His finger rubbed at the furrow between his eyebrows.

Yvie watched the expression of tiredness settle on his face. His other hand rested on the table and she knew a sudden urge to cover that hand with her own.

'Did you have a blank spot?' she asked softly.

Josh sighed again. 'Not exactly. I've just had things on my mind.' His eyes flashed over her and then away to settle on Tim as he fiddled with his camera.

Yvie followed his gaze.

'Tim got in with a bad lot at school and I suppose for a while we had a communication breakdown. We'd seemed to be getting on pretty well for a while after his . . .' He shrugged again. 'Well, he got behind with his schoolwork and I was only too pleased to have the chance to get him away from bad influences.'

Yvie nodded. 'He told me he had a lot of work to catch up on.'

Josh's eyes came back to her. 'He wasn't too keen on coming to San Francisco in the beginning and I didn't want to push him too hard. The past few years haven't been easy for him.' Josh rubbed his forehead again absently as his eyes looked into the past.

'He thought a lot of his grandmother, Renee's mother. He took her death pretty hard. His grandmother just about raised him.' Josh's face took on a bleak pinched look. 'God knows, Renee showed precious little interest in him and I, well, my job kept me away more than it should have so I have to take part of the blame.'

'When did she . . . when did his grandmother die?' Yvie asked.

'Four years ago,' he told her absently.

Four years ago. Yvie shied away from that and

they both sat in silence again. No one could say the conversation was flowing freely, Yvie thought wryly. She was ill-at-ease with him, unable to relax and she wished she could be as blasé about the situation as some of the other girls she knew would be. One particular girl in the office seemed to have a string of ex-boyfriends who were still her good friends.

Yvie glanced quickly across at Josh. No, she could never be his friend. Too much had gone before and it had run far too deeply.

'How much more of your book do you have to do?' Yvie asked uneasily. His book seemed to be the only safe subject between them now that they'd established that Dan wasn't guiding her questions.

For a moment she wondered if he had heard her for he didn't immediately reply.

'A couple of chapters,' he said eventually. 'If I can keep it flowing the way it has been these past few days I'll have it completed in a couple of weeks at the most.'

'That's good,' Yvie commented inadequately and she shifted in her seat.

'I suppose I have a sort of love-hate relationship with each one,' he expanded. 'I love the beginning because the challenge is before me but by the time I get to the end I'm so hyped-up I find it hard to wind down with nothing left to work on.'

'I've, uh, I've enjoyed all of your books very much,' Yvie volunteered a trifle embarrassedly.

Josh looked across at her and smiled crookedly. 'Thank you.'

'No. Really. I mean it. I have enjoyed them. They're easy to read, they flow, and the pace is fantastic. I . . . I have copies of them all,' she finished.

Josh inclined his head. 'I've been lucky. My gamble, throwing in my job with the paper, paid off I guess.'

'I guess it did.' Yvie smiled faintly as she remembered her father saying just that after he'd finished reading Josh's first book, in fact, the only book of Josh's he'd lived to read. 'Dad said as much, too,' she told him. 'He was full of praise for "The Constantine Conspiracy".'

'The first one. That's my favourite too.' His eyes held hers. 'For obvious reasons.'

Yvie dragged her eyes away from his. Obvious reasons? Well, they weren't obvious to her. She wouldn't let them be.

'I suppose most writers have a sentimental feeling for their first books,' she said evenly.

'Yvie.' His tone was softly caressing. 'Yvie, look at me.'

His hand encircled her arm as it lay on the table and of their own accord her eyes moved back to obey his gently compelling command.

'The book means more to me because I wrote it with you,' he said thickly.

'Josh, don't be ridiculous.' She gave a short laugh.

'I wrote it at the coast when we were together.'

Yvie wanted to crush her hands over her ears, shut out his words.

'You were with that book every step of the way, every chapter, every word of it,' he continued.

'Josh, please. Don't——'

'Don't what?'

'Don't!' Yvie appealed to him.

'Don't pretend we didn't have——'

'An affair,' she broke in punishingly, finishing his sentence with brutal determination. 'An affair, Josh. A cheap sordid affair. That's all we had.'

His fingers tightened painfully on her arm, bruising her flesh. 'Don't say that! You don't even believe it,' he growled tersely.

'Don't I? I think I do.' Yvie tried unsuccessfully to pull her arm from his grasp.

'Yvie, you're wrong,' he began.

'Am I? Oh, no, I'm not wrong. I had it all made perfectly clear to me four years ago.' She raised her eyes to look steadily into his. 'I had an affair with a married man. Nothing you can say now will change that, Josh. Now, please let go of my arm.'

CHAPTER FIVE

IF anything Josh's fingers tightened.

'Yvie, you didn't understand the situation,' he said angrily.

'Oh, I understood all right. You couldn't have put it more plainly.' Yvie was equally angry and she tried once again to free her arm from his vice-like grip. 'You had finished your book so you went back to your wife.'

'It wasn't like that at all. Look, Yvie——'

'Dad! Yvie!' They both turned to face Tim and a flash bulb momentarily blinded them as he snapped the shutter.

Tim grinned at them as he lowered the camera a little. 'Well, that was candid but how about a smile this time.'

'Tim!' Josh began, barely disguising his exasperation.

'Oh, come on, Dad! Just one shot. It's the end of the film and I want to get it developed,' Tim appealed to him.

'All right.' Josh sighed. 'But get it over with, will you?'

The camera flashed again and Yvie tried to relax her tensed facial muscles. Her smile had felt like little more than a grimace and she glanced down to see that Josh still had hold of her arm. Her eyes met his and went pointedly back to her arm. Slowly Josh released her but she could still feel the pressure of his fingers where they'd bruised her flesh and his eyes told her that as far as he was concerned the matter had only been shelved.

They left the restaurant not long after that, neither Josh nor Yvie making any attempt to prolong the evening, and Yvie had to restrain herself from racing the car madly back to the house. But she drove sedately enough, relief washing over her as she drew the car to a halt in the garage.

Josh climbed lithely from the front seat and switched on the overhead light before striding around to open Yvie's door. The confining space of the garage brought his body agonisingly close to her as she slipped past him and walked to the front of the car. The door to her flat, and sanctuary, was so close she had to tense herself not to dive inside without a backward glance.

'It was a great night, wasn't it, Yvie?' Tim walked up to her. 'Thanks for taking us.'

'That's all right. I enjoyed it, too.' The blatant lie came uneasily and guilt burned inside her as she looked away from Tim's smiling face. If only . . . Yvie drew herself together.

'Want another game of table tennis?' Tim asked hopefully. 'Good exercise after the meal.' He patted his tummy and Yvie felt her lips lift in an almost spontaneous smile.

'No, thanks. I don't think I'm quite up to any healthy exercise just at the moment. Relaxing with a book is about all I'll be able to manage right now.'

'How about you, Dad?' Tim turned slightly

towards his father as Josh walked up to stand beside Yvie.

She could feel him there, and her body responded instinctively to his nearness.

'Not for me, Tim.' His voice seemed to echo resonantly in the closed-in garage. 'I'm going to plead advanced age.'

'Oh, well.' Tim sighed heavily. 'I wonder what's on television.'

'I've got a programme. I'll get it for you,' Yvie offered and unlocked the door of her flat. Inside she crossed to pick up the magazine featuring the week's television programme and turned back to hand it to Tim who had followed her into the flat. Josh stood in the doorway.

'Thanks.' Tim leafed through the pages until he found Saturday's schedule. 'Sure you won't need it?'

'No.' Yvie shook her head.

'Let's see.' Tim glanced at his watch. ' "Star Trek" starts in five minutes. Wonder if I've seen it.'

He walked to the door and Josh stepped aside to let him though.

'Night, Yvie.' Tim lifted a hand in a half wave. 'Coming, Dad?'

'Yes, in a moment. I'll see you upstairs in a few minutes.' Josh watched as Tim bounded up the steps to the house before he slowly turned back into the flat, his eyes finding and holding Yvie's.

He stood just inside the door after he'd quietly closed it behind him, and he thrust his hands into the pockets of his trousers. His suit jacket was undone and the fine material of his shirt strained across the breadth of his chest. His hands in his pockets did the same thing to the material of his pants, moulding his thighs, and Yvie's mouth went dry, her muscles beginning to ache with tension.

She couldn't take this. She couldn't cope with being alone with him. It was a pain she found herself unable to bear. He'd hurt her deeply, far too deeply to erase the scars, and she hated him. She hated him. And hated herself for still wanting him after all he'd done. Because she did want him. Her body was still physically tuned to his and her only protection was in keeping away from him.

Forcing herself to move Yvie turned to toss her evening bag on to the sofa and then wished she hadn't for at least her purse had been something to clutch, a solid object for her fingers to hold on to. With a composure she was far from feeling she lightly folded her arms and unconsciously lifted her chin.

'Josh, I think we should call it a night. Thank you for the meal, I enjoyed it, but I'm rather tired and I want to go to bed.'

The line of his mouth twisted cynically. 'God, I wish it was that simple,' he said thickly and Yvie felt a wave of heat wash her body as her nerve ends quivered in response to the obvious arousal in his tone.

'It's late and I . . .' Yvie swallowed convulsively as his eyes burned over her, touching on each secret place that only he could know about.

'And you want to go to bed,' he finished softly, silkily.

He took a step towards her and panic stricken Yvie almost sprang back from him. Josh stopped, poised like a lithe jungle cat ready to pounce, and his jaw tensed in anger. He swore under his breath.

'Yvie, for God's sake, do you know what you're doing to me?' The words rasped from him and Yvie stood transfixed, unable to answer him.

He gave a harsh laugh and turned from her, two long strides taking him to the glass picture window overlooking the bay. His back and shoulders were tight, held tensely, and he raked a distracted hand through his fair hair.

'You have to know.' He spun around to face her again and even in her stunned shock her eyes went to the lock of hair that now raked across his forehead and she wanted to reach out and touch its remembered softness.

'Aren't I right, Yvie?' he asked harshly. 'You do know. And I'd hazard a guess that you're taking great delight in it.'

'What do you mean by that?' The question was a broken whisper.

'That you're getting some sort of perverse enjoyment out of holding me off.' He walked across to stand in front of her. 'Well? Haven't I hit the target, Yvie? You want to see me suffer a little, to pay me back for something I've supposedly done.'

'Supposedly done?' Yvie mouthed the words but no sound escaped her. 'Supposedly done?' she repeated and this time her voice came out high and sharp. 'My God, you've got some nerve. You come to San Francisco, apparently knowing

I'm here, expecting me to fall into your arms, worship at the feet of the great, the now famous Josh Graham, and when you find I won't play your game you accuse me of some infantile ploy. Well, it's not a game, Josh. It never was to me.'

'Yvie——' Josh took another step forward and she jerked back from him, her legs coming up against the sofa.

'If you're suffering then that's fine by me. As far as I'm concerned you couldn't suffer enough.'

'Yvie, for God's sake!' He reached out to clasp her arms but she drew as far back from him as the sofa would allow.

'Don't touch me!' Yvie's eyes were coldly withering. 'Unless you expect some reward for dinner this evening,' she threw at him. 'Because if that's the case then I'll pay for my own. I'm not in the habit of coming across on those terms.'

His face, burning with a smouldering anger that was barely contained, told her she had gone too far.

'And I'm not in the habit of expecting payment for a meal. And nor do I need to.' His lips thinned cruelly. 'But then there's always a first time for everything, isn't there?'

In one stride he was on her, his fingers biting into the flesh of her arms sliding around her to enclose her in a vice-like grip.

Her body met his, all solid masculine muscle. The softness of her breasts were crushed against his rock-hard chest and as thigh met thigh her traitorous body succumbed with an ease that shocked her to her very core. For four years she had fought to forget the fantastic feel of his body against hers but in those agonising seconds she realised that none of it was forgotten, that it had been merely hidden away, and she remembered him with total clarity.

She knew every last contour of him, the heady thumping of his heart in his solid chest, the flatness of his stomach, the exquisite surge within her as she felt the strength of his arousal.

Memory flooded forward to engulf her as his lips claimed hers, searing her with the burning hunger of his angry possession. And it was no gentle possession this. His lips plundered hers, forcing her mouth open, ravaging the softness within.

Yvie's response rose to meet him, casting aside all that had gone before. It was as though her body had lain dormant, hibernated, waiting for his touch to awaken her, for the exhilarating feel of his lips on hers, and the fire smouldered deep inside her, flaring, a craving for complete capitulation.

The timbre of Josh's kisses slowly changed, the anger leaving him to be replaced by a more persuasive demand. His lips surrendered hers, to slide along her jawline finding a sensitive spot behind her ear and a low moan rumbled from deep in his chest.

'Yvie! Yvie! You feel so good.' His breath fanned her ear sending quivers of delight down her spine. 'This is how I remembered it was with us. It always was. We're two halves of one whole. We always will be.'

He was right about that and deep down she knew it. When they came together they moulded as one. And it *did* feel so good. As though she was back where she belonged. After so long. Far too long. They might never have been apart and nothing had happened in between. She'd never married Larry and . . .

Josh's lips gently probed the hollow at the base of her throat and Yvie's fingers weaved through the soft strands of his hair.

Poor Larry. No wonder their marriage had been doomed before it even began.

Yvie moaned lowly as Josh's lips stole lower skimming tantalisingly along the neckline of her dress across the mound of one breast and then the other.

She knew she'd hurt Larry and . . . Oh, my God! A cold hand of guilt clutched at her stomach and began to spread through her entire body. She'd been totally unfair to Larry and all because of Josh Graham. Now here she was allowing him to make love to her. And he thought she was still married.

'No! Please! No!' The choked words broke from her and her hands pushed against Josh's shoulders.

His arms about her held her fast and his blue eyes, almost black with passion, rose to meet hers.

'Please, Josh, let me go. I don't want this.' Her fingers made no impression on the solidness of his chest.

'You don't mean that,' he said softly, disbelieving.

'I do! I do!' She continued to push him away from her but he refused to let her go.

The pressure of his thighs stirred against her and she caught her breath at the answering torrent within her.

'Josh, I can't,' she pleaded.

'Can't or won't?' he asked harshly.

'Can't and won't.' She replied softly and firmly as she stood quietly now in the circle of his arms, having exerted an iron control over herself.

Josh slowly let her go. 'You took your time deciding.'

They faced each other and he didn't attempt to disguise his arousal. Yvie's legs were weak beneath her, in danger of giving way on her.

'I . . . you . . . Larry,' she began incoherently.

At the mention of Larry's name Josh's head went up, his eyes narrowing as they bored into her. 'It's a little late to start thinking about your husband, isn't it?' he asked harshly and Yvie wrapped her arms about her body seeking some defence against his mocking gaze.

'I think you'd better go,' she said softly.

'How long has he been away?' The question was almost insolent and Yvie shrugged. 'Too long apparently,' Josh added cruelly. 'If your response is any indication.'

He turned on his heel and left her then and Yvie stood numbly looking at the door as it closed behind him.

Somehow Yvie managed to undress and crawl into bed. She lay there wide-eyed staring unseeingly at the darkened ceiling and for what seemed like hours she felt nothing, no emotion whatsoever. She couldn't even feel revulsion at her perfidious response to Josh's kisses.

His kisses and caresses had aroused her just the way they used to and she knew she hadn't wanted him to stop, no matter what she had said to the contrary. She'd wanted him to go on making love to her and she knew how wonderful it would have been. It always had been good between them.

The pain began then, clutching deep inside her to rise and engulf her and she closed her eyes, squeezing them tightly shut to try to blot out his image. But that was impossible to do. His face was engraved in her memory forever and his touch was burned upon her skin like an invisible brand.

It took her ages to achieve the oblivion of sleep and she woke early feeling headachey and sluggish. The thought of food nauseated her but she forced down a slice of toast with her cup of tea.

All the while her eyes rose nervously to the ceiling. There was no sound from above but she knew he was there, so close. And after last night she knew he was far too close. She had to get away, at least for today, and put some breathing space between herself and the pure torture of his proximity.

She'd drive out of the city, get into the fresh air of the open countryside. Yvie sighed. But then there was the battle with the returning traffic and she didn't quite feel up to coping with that today.

Perhaps she could ring Abby and see if she was free for the afternoon. They could go somewhere together. But she wasn't really in a good company mood. Feeling as she did now she'd only mope about and that wouldn't be fair on Abby. No, she'd be better off on her own.

The park. Of course. She'd take a picnic lunch and sit in the park. She often did that when the weather was fine, as it was today.

With her mind made up on a chosen course the day looked just a little brighter and she set about finishing a few chores before she packed herself a crisp fresh salad. Picking up her travelling rug, a soft pillow and a book she'd been promising herself she'd read for ages, she was ready to go.

Juggling everything in her arms she quietly opened the door into the garage, half expecting Tim to be there but the garage was deserted, and she quickly threw everything into the car and drove away from the house.

When she reached the bottom of the street she gradually exhaled the breath she'd been holding. She was away. Free of Josh Graham's potent nearness.

She drove slowly enjoying the pleasantness of her lack of haste. Eventually she reached her favourite park and pulled off the road into a vacant parking bay.

A few people were there before her, a couple of physical fitness devotees were jogging or performing callisthenics and a number of families were gathered together. One group had already embarked on an enthusiastic game of baseball.

Yvie selected a grassy patch beneath a tree that would still afford shade as the sun shifted and spreading out her rug she flopped down on it. It was far too early for lunch and so she picked up her book. But the family of baseballers caught more of her attention and she was happy to sit and watch them, letting the fine clear day seep inside her, relaxing her. Eventually she lay back on her pillow and lifted her book again.

It was really a very good story, Yvie discovered, romantic suspense, and she was able to push everything out of her mind and become engrossed in the tale. Just getting away from the house was proving to be amazingly reviving. Things fell into the right perspective somehow. Yvie shifted into a more comfortable position and sighed pleasurably as she read on.

A deep masculine voice made her jump and she dropped her book as she gazed upwards. Her heartbeats raced and she felt herself pale. Pain jabbed through her and she fought down the urge to scramble to her feet and run.

For one moment, with the sun behind him, she had mistakenly thought the tall fair young man standing over her was Josh. He was as broad and as fit-looking as Josh was, but he was a good ten years younger.

'Sorry I startled you,' he said genuinely. 'I didn't realise you hadn't seen me approaching.'

He smiled easily and Yvie retrieved her paperback and began leafing through the pages for her place. If she ignored him he'd go away.

'Is it a good book?' he asked, cocking his head so that he could read the title.

'Yes, it is,' she replied stiffly and shifted her gaze pointedly back to the page. She had no desire to start up a conversation with anyone, let alone a young man so obviously on the make.

'And you don't feel like talking?' he grimaced ruefully, taking her freeze-off in good part.

'No,' she said and added a little less stringently. 'I'm sorry.'

'Me too.' He shrugged, his eyes travelling over her reclining figure in cool T-shirt and shorts. 'Maybe I'll see you here some other time.'

'Maybe,' Yvie mouthed flatly and he raised a hand and jogged on his way.

Yvie watched him go. Really, he was nothing at all like Josh, apart from his fair hair and height, and yet in those first few seconds her body had reacted in that same old way.

All her good work during the two years she'd been in San Francisco had crumbled as though it had never been. She had been certain it was all over, this thing she had, seeing Josh Graham in every tall fair man who happened along. In the beginning she would pass someone in the street and her breath would catch in her throat only to have her heart sink when she realised it wasn't Josh but a total stranger.

Now, today, she'd done the very same thing. It was starting all over. Yvie lowered her book and shielded her eyes with her arm resting across her forehead. The sudden sight of the young man standing gazing down at her had struck a chord in her memory and she was slowly being drawn back in time.

She was sunbathing on the beach in front of their cottage at Caloundra. She was stretched out on her back as she was now, her arm protecting her eyes from the sun. And she was wondering when Josh would be returning.

He'd been in Brisbane for four days and she'd missed him dreadfully. Somehow nothing seemed the same when he was away. The beach, the sky, the sunshine, it all paled without Josh.

It was just over a month now since Josh had moved into his unit along the beach and Yvie saw him almost every evening. During the day he worked on his book and after dinner he walked along the beach and called in to chat to her father or, if her father was tired, then Josh and Yvie beachcombed alone. They'd stroll in the moonlight arm in arm and before she went inside Josh would kiss her goodnight.

And how she'd yearned for those kisses, wanting so much more than that, his caresses setting her aflame. She knew he felt the same way, she knew he wanted her too, but Josh always drew back, sent her inside, and she had to be content with that.

Just lying on the beach thinking about him sent shivers of desire rushing through her. She wanted him to make love to her so very much. At first her own responses had shocked her, for she'd never felt this way before, this burning need, this craving for a satisfaction she knew he could give her.

She supposed at nineteen compared to her contemporaries she was extremely naïve about sex, but she'd never felt any great desire to surrender her body to any of the young men she'd known in the past. It had been no great hardship to fob them off if they became too persistent.

That's why her responses to Josh's lovemaking had initially overwhelmed her. She had suspected she was rather an oddity, or just plain undersexed, but Josh had proved her so very wrong. She loved him so much and to make love with him completely seemed as natural to her as breathing.

'Wake up, sleepy head.' His voice brought her out of her reflections and their very content made a blush wash over her.

'Josh! You're back,' she stated the obvious as she sat up.

He laughed softly. 'Mmm. Just got back half an hour ago so I came straight down to see you.'

His eyes moved openly down her figure clad in its modest bikini. Yvie felt hot all over and her eyes fell as he sat down beside her on the sand. She knew his eyes were still on her and her skin tingled as though he'd touched her.

'Did you have a good trip?' she asked, her heartbeats flipping madly in her chest. She ran her eyes over him, drinking in his handsomeness. He looked tired around the eyes and his mouth seemed a little drawn.

'Fine,' he replied but didn't elaborate.

His hand reached out, his fingers clasping hers where they lay on her bare leg and his thumb softly caressed her palm.

'I missed you.' His voice seemed to come from deep in his chest and his eyes burned into hers.

Yvie's heart felt as though it had turned completely over and then raced as his eyes moved over her face to settle on the tremble of her lips.

She swallowed painfully. 'I missed you, too,' she whispered back, her love for him shining in her eyes.

Josh caught his breath and slowly raised her hand to his lips, softly kissing the sunwarmed skin.

The air between them crackled, surrounding them in the circle of its turbulence, isolating them in a small world of their own so that they were totally alone to each other. And they sat like that intent only on each other until the raucous cry of a seagull overhead brought reality back to them. Josh was the first to break their silence.

'I'd also like to invite you and your father to dinner at my place tonight,' he smiled at her. 'After all, I've eaten here often enough. It's time I returned the favour. Are you game to try my cooking?'

'Oh, Josh, Dad's got a friend coming over this evening, an old crony of his. They play cards for a few hours,' she told him regretfully. 'But I could come,' she added and then blushed at her presumptuousness. 'I'm sorry. I ... maybe we could come another night.'

'You can come if you'd like to,' Josh grinned. 'Unless your father expects you to play cards as well.'

'Oh, no. I don't play with them,' she hastened to assure him. 'I usually read or watch television.'

'Okay then. I'll pick you up at, say, six-thirty?' He glanced at his wristwatch. 'And as time's moving on and I'll need to do some slaving over a hot stove, I'd better be going.'

He stood up and taking Yvie's hand again he drew her up beside him, smiling down at her.

'Until tonight,' he said softly and then walked quickly away along the beach.

Yvie was in a quandary over what to wear. Slacks and a nice blouse? No. A dress would be more feminine. She finally decided on a pale lemon one in soft light cheesecloth. It had short sleeves and the neckline was gathered by a white cord drawstring.

Slipping it over her head she tied the matching white cord belt around her waist. The lemon shade of the dress accentuated her deep tan and she brushed her fair hair until it shone. Carefully she applied her makeup and once satisfied with the results she stepped into her high heeled sandals and walked through to the living room.

'You look very nice, love.' Her father smiled at her as he threw a plain cloth over the card table. 'Where's Josh taking you to dinner?'

Yvie hadn't told her father that the meal was to be at Josh's unit and as she hesitated before answering him both Josh and her father's friend arrived. In the flurry of introductions and small talk Yvie left her father's question unanswered, convincing herself that she wasn't deceiving him, that she'd tell him tomorrow. She wanted tonight to be hers and Josh's

CHAPTER SIX

JOSH's unit was on the eighth floor of the apartment building on the foreshore and from the balcony the view took in stretches of beach, the ever changing Spit to the left and Bribie Island to the right. Josh fixed them drinks and they sat on the balcony watching the colour changes over the water as the sun sank behind them over the Glasshouse Mountains. They chatted companionably enough but they were too far apart for Yvie. Josh sat in his own chair away from hers and she yearned for him to touch her, to hold her in his arms.

Perhaps she should make the first move. But no, she couldn't. Suddenly he was so much the man of the world while she, she felt as gauche as a schoolgirl.

Did he regret those fervent kisses they'd shared on the moonlit beach? Had he simply been amusing himself and was he now tired of the game? Was it his way of crying off? But only hours ago he had told her he missed her.

She stole a glance at him but could glean nothing from his profile as he sat watching a container ship move along the passage out to sea. Had she mistakenly read too much into their relationship? The more she dwelt on that question the more unsure of herself she felt and she had to struggle to make conversation.

She could barely conceal her relief when Josh suggested they go inside and eat.

It seemed to Yvie he took great pains not to touch her, standing back while she preceded him into the living room, although he held her chair for her before he went into the kitchen for the deliciously aromatic meal. Of course the food was divine and yet Yvie couldn't do it full justice. What they talked about she couldn't afterwards have told.

As the evening wore on Yvie sank into the depths of depression and it seemed to her that Josh became more and more distant. When they finished the meal he refused her offer of help with the dishes saying he'd attend to them later and they carried their coffee into the living room.

It was a small intimate room, tastefully furnished, and Josh switched on the stereo, turning the volume down so that the soft strings didn't intrude on their conversation. On their attempt at conversation, Yvie thought miserably. By nine thirty her nerves had reached screaming pitch and her body ached with tension.

'Yvie!'

She drew her mind back from its tortured self-disparagement and knew Josh had had to speak her name more than once to get her attention.

'Oh, yes. I'm sorry,' she stammered miserably.

A small frown puckered Josh's brow and he stood up, hands shoved into the pockets of his slacks. He prowled restlessly across to stand in front of the sliding glass doors on to the balcony. Slowly he turned back to face her.

'This isn't working, is it?' he asked flatly and

Yvie could only stare up at him wide-eyed and wretched. 'I knew it was a mistake. I was a bloody fool to think I could . . .' he stopped and turned away from her again.

Yvie got shakily to her feet. She had never felt so despairing in her life. A tight ball of tears gathered in her throat, almost choking her, and she swallowed convulsively.

'I think I should go,' she managed to get out at last in a tight voice that was far removed from her own. 'I . . . you needn't see me out. I'll just . . .' She turned away, fumbling for her bag and the light shawl that she'd left on the coffee table. She started for the door, her eyes blurring now with unshed tears. She wouldn't allow herself to cry. Not in front of Josh.

So intent on reaching the door was she that she didn't hear his footfalls on the carpet, but he was suddenly beside her, strong fingers encircling her arm, gently halting her progress, turning her slowly but firmly to face him.

'Yvie, you can't walk home by yourself. If you want to go I'll drive you.'

Her eyes were on the V-neck of his brown knit shirt, fixed on the tiny curls of fair hair that showed there. Had he left her a choice?

'It doesn't matter, Josh. I can walk. Honestly. I'm sorry about this evening, if I've . . .' She swallowed painfully, blinking back the tears that threatened more than ever to fall.

'Oh, Yvie.' His fingers lifted her chin and a tear spilled over on to her cheek.

Yvie closed her eyes in mortification and tried to pull away from him. If she didn't go now she'd end up making a complete fool of herself.

Josh said something under his breath, something she couldn't catch, and then his arms were around her, holding her to him.

'Yvie! Yvie!' he murmured into her hair. 'I've made a complete mess of this evening, haven't I?' He leaned back and regarded her broodingly.

His gaze roved over her face, her brow, her nose, the blueness of his eyes deepening to lustrous black as they settled on her lips. Slowly, as though he was waging a war within himself and losing the battle, his head came down and he put his mouth to hers.

His kisses were light, softly tantalising, moving deliciously on her lips, exciting a spontaneous response that Yvie was incapable of quelling and the eagerness of her reaction aroused Josh so that his kisses hardened, and their bodies strained against each other.

Yvie moved against him knowing he was as totally aroused as she was and she gave free rein to the surge of desire that grew inside her. The unhappiness of the evening faded as though it had never been, for somehow she felt rather that she had come safely home.

Josh moaned brokenly. 'Yvie, we have to stop this.'

She burrowed her head into his shoulder, her lips leaving soft kisses along his throat to his earlobe.

'Oh, Josh, it feels so good.'

'I know. *Too* good.' His voice dropped, his deep heightened tone sending shivers of delight through her.

The burning expression on his face made her drop her gaze and she gave a soft shaky laugh.

'I thought you were tired of me, that I was boring you,' she said breathlessly.

'Never.' His firm denial left her in no doubt that she was mistaken. 'You could never do that.'

Yvie glanced up at him, her gaze drinking in his still darkened eyes, the softened line of his lips. 'Why were you so distant tonight? You didn't even kiss me when we arrived.'

'You don't know how much I wanted to, believe me, but I was trying to keep everything light. I knew if I touched you we'd end up like this.' He sighed unevenly. 'God, Yvie, you're so young and I'm so much older than you are.'

'Twelve years isn't too much and, well, I don't think you're old at all. Not to me, you're not.' She touched his lips lightly with one finger and his mouth closed on it, his teeth gently nibbling on her fingertip.

'I was a fool, wasn't I, to think I could bring you here and keep my hands to myself?' His fingers played over her back. 'I've been wanting to hold you like this all night.'

Yvie slid her own fingers beneath the waistband of his shirt, delighting in the feel of his skin, warm to her touch.

His eyes burned down into hers. 'Yvie, don't look at me like that,' he got out raggedly.

'Like what?' A tiny teasing smile touched the corners of her mouth.

'Like that,' he repeated. 'Or I won't be able to let you go tonight.'

Yvie slid closer to him. 'I don't think I want you to,' she whispered.

His arms tightened momentarily and then he put her away from him.

'Do you want a drink? I could sure use one.' He ran a hand through his hair and crossed to the small side bar. He poured himself a scotch and added ginger ale to Yvie's, walking back to hand her the glass.

Taking a mouthful of his drink he turned and sank into an easy chair motioning Yvie to the one opposite him. She walked past the one he indicated, sitting down beside him, her thigh touching his.

'Yvie——' he began.

'Oh, Josh, please. I can't bear not to be close to you.'

She looked up at him beseechingly and Josh sighed in resignation, the corners of his mouth lifting. Taking her glass from her he set it beside his on the coffee table and pulled her on to his lap.

'I hope you realise you're playing with fire,' he murmured softly as his lips caressed the curve of her neck.

'I only have to think of you to do that,' she told him honestly and Josh lifted his head to look into her eyes.

He shook his head almost imperceptibly. Yvie put her hands on either side of his face and lowered her lips to his. For a split second he remained motionless and then with a broken moan that seemed to echo deep in his chest he crushed her into his arms, his hard demanding kisses finding an answering ardour in Yvie.

Her fingers slid beneath the collar of his shirt to stroke the back of his neck. Josh found the tie cord on her dress, undoing it and widening the neckline so that he could push the soft material off her shoulders, his caressing fingers sliding downwards to cover her breasts. His lips moved sensuously over her shoulders as he reached around to unclasp her lacy bra.

As the soft light fell on her naked breasts he caught his breath and then slowly lowered his lips to kiss first one aroused peak and then the other. A wild abandoned excitement rose in Yvie and she moaned deep in her throat, her fingers sliding into his hair, cradling his head to her body.

And her body ached for him, yearned for more than this tempting rapture, and her hands slid beneath his shirt over the damp smoothness of his skin. Her fingers lifted his shirt, and he raised his arms to shrug it off. Now the softness of her breasts tingled against the bareness of his hair-roughened chest.

The last of Yvie's inhibitions faded away as Josh's nearness aroused her even more. And she wanted him closer. This was the man she loved and she wanted him desperately.

Her fingers slid tremblingly downwards to the buckle of his belt, undid it, and reached for the press stud at the waist of his slacks. Josh's fingers covered hers.

'Yvie,' he said thickly. 'Do you know what you're inviting?'

'Yes.' She nodded. 'I love you, Josh.'

Josh closed his eyes and rested his head back against the chair for a moment. 'Yvie, if we take this any further I won't be able to keep my head.'

Yvie applied a little more pressure to the press stud and it pulled apart with a snap that seemed to echo loudly in the room. Their eyes met, held, burned with their mutal desire, and Yvie's fingers slid lower to his zipper, drawing it slowly downwards.

For a split second she thought he was going to stop her, put her from him, but then he was crushing her to him, his hands playing down along the length of her spine. In no time the remainder of their clothing had been discarded and Josh lifted her into his arms, carrying her into his bedroom, laying her on the bed, the long lithe length of him following her.

His naked body felt smooth and warm where it touched hers and the curves and planes of his muscular form were highlighted by the lamplight streaming in through the open doorway.

Josh kissed her with deep slowness, his hands moving over her full breasts rekindling her fire. His fingers slid lower over her flat stomach finding each secret place that only he had explored.

There was an instant when he would have pulled back, when he realised he was the first, but Yvie's arms tightened around him, and then it was far too late to stop, even if either of them had wanted to. Yvie didn't. Not for a moment. Josh's lovemaking showed her another facet of herself, one she hadn't even suspected existed within her. Her heart swelled with her love for him as he lifted her higher in a cascade of earthshattering ecstasy.

When their ragged breathing had slowed, Josh lifted himself away from her to lie beside her, pulling her into the circle of his arm, settling her head on his shoulder. Yvie's eyes roved over him dreamily and she placed a quick contented kiss against the line of his jaw. He turned towards her, the corners of his mouth lifting in a smile and his hand cupped her cheek as he moved to kiss her tenderly on the lips.

'You're beautiful,' he said huskily and at that moment she felt beautiful, as though she was the most desirable woman on earth.

'So are you,' she laughed softly and ran her hand audaciously downwards over the flatness of his stomach. She felt him quiver and he covered her hand with his, raising it to his lips.

'Did I hurt you?' he asked throatily, a frown of concern on his brow.

Yvie shook her head. 'Only briefly. You were wonderful.'

He gave a half laugh, and she wondered if she'd disconcerted him for a dull flush momentarily coloured his face, and then he sobered.

'Yvie, I didn't plan on allowing this to happen tonight. In fact, I was guarding against it.' He grimaced slightly.

'Why?' she asked him, her body instantaneously still.

He must have sensed her sudden tension for he drew her closer. 'Not because I didn't want it to happen, believe me. God knows, I've wanted to make love to you from the moment I saw you.'

'I don't understand, Josh?' Yvie swallowed.

He was silent for a moment. 'Yvie, have you thought about the consequences?'

She regarded him levelly. 'You mean I could become pregnant?' She said quietly, flushing as a tiny shaft of delight surged through her. To have Josh's child would be marvellous, the ultimate expression of their love.

'I don't suppose you've——' He stopped as though searching for the right words.

'Taken precautions?' she finished for him and shook her head, not looking at him. 'There was never any need to, before.'

His hand ran lightly over her hip and down her thigh. 'I'll take care of it in future,' he said his lips touching her shoulder, moving downwards, and Yvie shivered, smiling with pleasure as her hands luxuriated in the softness of his hair.

He lifted his head, resting on one elbow as he looked down at her, his eyes darkening with renewed desire. 'I should say this won't happen again but I know it will. It can't seem to keep my cool when you're around. But seeing you like this,' his hand caressed the mound of her naked breast that swelled to his touch, 'plays havoc with my good intentions.'

His lips came down to cover hers and Yvie's body arched to meet his as their passion rose again. And it was very late when Yvie tiptoed into the cottage and slid into her own narrow bed.

On her blanket in the park half the world away from that night, Yvie stirred fitfully as her memories taunted her. That night, their coming together, had been so wonderful, the fulfilment of all her dreams, the first of many nights they'd shared. They couldn't get enough of each other.

Yvie's lips twisted. 'I'll take care of it in future,' he'd said that first night. But by then the damage had been done. The pain began again and Yvie sat up swiftly. She wouldn't think about that, she couldn't allow herself to think about it for that was one part of the past she kept firmly shut away. She'd made herself a promise that she'd never let that particular memory torture her again. The scar ran far too deeply.

The family of baseballers had given up their game and retired to the shade of the trees, the womenfolk busily passing out the lunch. Yvie glanced at her watch. It was after twelve so she supposed she should eat as well. Reaching for her picnic basket she set out her salad and sighed unenthusiastically. She wasn't in the least bit hungry for her stomach felt tight and tense but she made herself go through the motions of eating and she was relieved when she could tidy away and close the picnic hamper.

She drained the remainder of her soft drink and put the empty can aside to go in the trash can. Desultorily she gazed around her as she held her book on her lap not in any hurry to get back to it for her memories had unsettled her once again.

The baseballers were all reclining after their meal, obviously replete, and even the joggers had gone or were resting.

Yvie was suddenly filled with despair. Josh had been here less than a week and had wreaked absolute havoc on her. She just couldn't see herself coping with the long weeks ahead. If only Dan hadn't lent him the house. Dan was too friendly by far, too easy going. Especially when the person involved was one of their top authors, probably their very top author, Yvie reflected wryly.

Closing her eyes, she bit gently on her bottom lip. Why, oh, why, she appealed once again, didn't Josh Graham change publishers when he'd had the chance? Although Dan was moderately well established his publishing firm could hardly be called well known. Why. . .? But there was nothing to be gained by going over it all again. Some cruel trick of fate had decreed that Josh stay with Dan's outfit, bringing their paths into contact once again.

'Sleeping Beauty, as I live and breathe.' A warm hand ran teasingly up Yvie's bare leg, stopping at the knee and squeezing gently.

Yvie's eyes flew open and she blinked sleepily. 'Paul.' She sat up, rubbing her eyes. 'What are you doing here?' she asked bewilderedly.

'Looking for you,' he grinned, white teeth flashing against his olive skin.

'But how did you know I was here?' Yvie had dozed off and was having trouble orientating herself.

Paul shrugged. 'I went by your flat and no one knew where you were. Then I remembered Abby saying you sometimes came here and,' he raised his hands, 'there was a car just like yours, so here I am. Once inside the park I just looked for the most sexy girl around and spied you immediately.'

Yvie smiled, unable to stop herself.

'There!' Paul touched her cheek. 'You're smiling. You must be pleased to see me.'

Yvie was having trouble getting her mind into gear. Then one point screamed out at her. If Paul had been to her flat . . .

'You called at my place?' she asked him evenly.

'Yes. And I met your Josh Graham and his son. The boy told me he'd seen you drive away early this morning.' Paul grimaced. 'Can't say I got an especially warm welcome from our writer. I must have interrupted his train of thought. Even after I explained I worked with you he didn't thaw. Talk about freezing. Is he the silent moody type?'

'No, I don't think so,' Yvie stammered. 'Perhaps you did interrupt his writing.'

Paul sighed. 'I'd better keep out of his way when he comes to the office.' His frown cleared and he beamed at her. 'But let's not talk about work, it's the weekend. I'm glad I found you, Yvie.' He gave her his best smile and Yvie had to admit he was charm personified.

'What happened to the lovely lass you were wining, dining, etc., this weekend?' she asked, moving over so he could sit down on the blanket beside her.

'Yvie, what makes you think there was any other lady?' he appealed to her.

Yvie smiled knowingly.

'Okay.' Paul gave in gracefully. 'She turned out to be a not-so-lovely lady. We had a disagreement.'

'I see.' Yvie tried not to laugh.

'Yvie, have pity. I'm bruised. I need the arms of a sympathetic woman.'

She did laugh then and Paul joined in.

'Seriously, love, I came to see if you'd have dinner with me this evening. I didn't feel like eating alone.' He took hold of her hand.

Yvie hesitated. 'I don't know, Paul.'

'Come on. What's wrong with two friends having a meal together.' He squeezed her hand.

'Nothing, I suppose.' What was there at the flat for her anyway? She'd only sit nervously wondering if Josh would come down. 'All right, Paul. I'd like that.'

'Great.' He beamed. 'Let's go then.'

'But I'm not dressed,' she protested as he pulled her to her feet.

'We'll go via your flat and you can change.'

'It's too early, isn't it?' Yvie glanced down at her watch. 'Good grief! I must have slept for hours.' Now that she took notice the shadows had shifted.

'Fantastic! You'll be all bright-eyed. We can party all night.'

'Oh, no. No partying. You said dinner,' Yvie reminded him.

'Okay. Just dinner.' Paul grinned. 'How about Fisherman's Wharf?'

'Oh, Paul, I don't really think I feel hungry enough to do justice to a fancy restaurant.'

'No, I guess I don't either.' Paul gave it some thought. 'I know this casual little place in the Cannery. They make great hamburgers.'

'That sounds fine.' Yvie smiled.

'Right. Let's go.' He helped her fold the rug

and carried the picnic basket to the car. 'I'll follow you home, seeing as I don't have to change into my fancy restaurant gear,' he laughed as he waved and walked along the road to where he'd left his car.

Yvie turned her Pinto and headed towards Sausalito. She left the garage door up and she was just climbing out of the car when Paul pulled into the driveway behind her.

'Very sedate driving, Miss Dean,' Paul grinned as he followed her into the flat and gazed around appreciatively. 'Always love this place. It makes my flat look very bachelorish.'

'Bachelorish?' Yvie laughed softly, trying to dispel the inner tension that had gripped her as soon as she drove into the garage. Back here meant Josh was near.

'Yes, bachelorish. Kind of needs a woman's touch.' His eyes danced as he flung himself on to the sofa and settled his feet comfortably on the cofee table. 'And I bet when it comes to a woman's touch you're the greatest, Yvie.'

She turned her head to glance at him as she drew her slacks and shirt from her wardrobe and she knew she'd flushed slightly.

'Such flattery,' she quipped.

'But I meant it.' He flung his hands up theatrically and his bottom lip pouted. 'And you never take me seriously.'

Paul was nice and a good friend but she didn't believe for a moment that he was serious. She was always his sounding board when things went awry with one of his many romances. Besides, she wasn't his type. He preferred brunettes with long willowy legs and voluptuous figures.

'I seem to remember someone saying "never mix business with pleasure", when a certain young typist at the office made it obvious she couldn't resist your dark Italian eyes,' Yvie reminded him lightly.

'I said that?'

Yvie nodded.

He gave her statement a little thought. 'Obviously said in the heat of the moment. Strictly self-preservation,' he assured her.

'No doubt.' Yvie chuckled as she headed for the bathroom with her change of clothes. 'I won't be long. There are some magazines on the table beside you.'

'Don't want any help scrubbing your back?' he asked teasingly.

'No, thanks. I have a perfectly adequate brush.' She replied turning back to look at him as she opened the door.

'Rats! Foiled again.' He winked at her and picked up a magazine.

Yvie took a quick shower and slipped into her dark blue gaberdine slacks and loose pale blue towelling shirt. She used some light make-up and brushed her hair before rejoining Paul.

He put down the magazine he'd been reading and glanced at his watch. 'So quick? Wow! You are some lady, Yvie Dean. Why hasn't someone snapped you up?'

'Someone did.' She gave a half laugh that held no bitterness. 'And put me down again so let that be a warning to you.' Her lightness robbed the words of any underlying meaning and Paul smiled with her as they walked to his car.

'Unbelievable. The guy must have been nuts.'
He started the car and carefully negotiated the
steep driveway. 'You must have married pretty
young,' he remarked as he headed the car towards
the city.

Yvie paused before answering him. She never
spoke of the past to anyone. Not Dan or Abby.
And she didn't want to discuss it with Paul. She
felt him shoot her a sideways glance.

'Yes. I was twenty,' she replied reluctantly.

'What happened?' he asked, his voice gentle.

Yvie sat silently again her hands lying calmly in
her lap. What happened? What could she say? That
she'd married Larry for all the wrong reasons, all
purely selfish, with no thought of what she would
be doing to him. While Larry, Larry had been far
more understanding than she'd suspected he could
be. Far more understanding than she'd deserved.

'As you said, I was very young and it just
didn't work out,' she finished softly. A tiny pain
clutched at her heart and grew. Because I wasn't
free to marry anyone. My heart, my mind, my
body belonged to someone else. And I couldn't
forget him. Haven't forgotten.

'Pity,' Paul consoled, then changed the subject
easily, for which Yvie was profoundly grateful,
and by the time they reached the restaurant their
conversation was light, back to their usual casual
banter.

They enjoyed the light meal and it was almost
eleven o'clock by the time Paul pulled into the
driveway again. Only one window overhead
showed a light in the house and the glow fell out
on to the bonnet of the car lighting the interior.

'Thanks for a beaut evening, Paul.' Yvie had her hand on the door catch. 'I enjoyed it.'

'Me too,' he smiled at her. 'You're a restful person to be with, Yvie, and I needed that tonight.'

Yvie smiled back at him knowing for once he was being serious. He leaned across and touched a light kiss to her forehead.

'See you tomorrow at the office,' he said, not taking their goodnight any further.

Yvie nodded and climbed out of the car to stand watching him as he reversed out of the gates and drove away. Sighing, she opened her bag and searched for the garage remote control unit. It wasn't there and neither was the key to the outer door of her flat.

Oh, no! She searched frantically through her purse again but knew with a sinking feeling that the key was inside her work bag. But where was the remote unit? She cast her mind back to the afternoon. She remembered driving into the garage and then she'd put the small electronic unit on to the car seat in her hurry to get into her flat in case Josh came downstairs.

Her eyes rose to the lighted window. There was only one thing she could do. She'd have to get Josh to let her into the house. Her heartbeats raced, thumping in her chest, and she swallowed convulsively. At least he wasn't in bed. The light was burning in the study so he must still be working on his book.

On suddenly shaky legs she walked across to the outer door of the house. The ornate knocker thudded hollowly on the heavy door and the noise seemed to shout out into the darkness.

CHAPTER SEVEN

IT seemed hours before the light in the vestibule came on and then the door opened. Josh stood there in the frame of light and all the breath seemed to go out of Yvie. She couldn't get her lungs to inhale, her vocal chords to work and she struggled for breath.

He was so compellingly devastating standing there oozing pure animal magnetism, backlit, almost pagan, like some ancient, beautifully sculptured statue. His feet and chest were bare. All he wore was a pair of faded denims that hugged his thighs and hung low on his hips. His broad tanned shoulders glowed bronze beneath the light bulb and the curves and contours of his muscles were highlighted in a study of light and shade.

Her eyes drank him in, went from the matt of fair hair on his chest arrowing downwards, soft silvery strands disappearing beneath the waistband of his jeans. Yvie turned hot all over, her legs weakening as she was gripped by a purely physical ache of desire. In that moment she wanted him with a fire that raged out of control, its strength far greater than anything she'd known before.

Some of her feelings must have been reflected in her eyes for she sensed a tension enter his body and, as she dropped her lids to shield her eyes lest she give too much away, his fingers tightened his hold on the door frame. He made no attempt to speak, just stood very still waiting for her to make the first move.

And how she wished she could move, just step up to him, slide her arms about him, rest her body against his, and run her lips over the tanned tautness of his skin. If only she could. Yvie clutched desperately at her composure, struggling to regain at least an outward calm.

'I'm sorry. I hope I didn't interrupt your work but,' she swallowed, 'I've left my key inside.'

Josh's eyes were in too much shadow for her to be able to read their expression but she caught the glitter of their brightness as he watched her.

'No, you're not interrupting anything,' he said a trifle drily and stood back so that she could step into the vestibule.

And once inside the walls of the small entryway began to press in on her. Josh's body was a tantlisation, far too close for her peace of mind. She stepped quickly to the stairs and began to mount them with quick jerky movements. His bare feet made no sound on the carpeted treads but she knew he moved close behind her and her back prickled with her awareness of him. If she stopped . . .

She almost bolted up the last few steps and she began to stride along the hallway towards the door that opened on to the steps leading back into the garage. The light from the open study doorway illuminated the hallway.

'Yvie,' he said softly behind her and her step faltered.

She took a couple of paces and then turned to face him. 'Thanks for letting me in,' she began, a little breathless from her rush up the stairs. At least, she told herself that was the reason for her shortness of breath, her racing heart.

Josh shrugged, his hands on his lean hips. 'How about a cup of coffee. I'd just made some.'

'Oh, no. No, thanks. I . . . it's late and I have to work tomorrow.'

'I'd like to talk to you about that,' he said, his voice free of expression, 'and a cup of coffee won't keep you long.'

No, she screamed at herself. Keep clear of him. Remember what ends up happening every time you're alone with him. And tonight he seemed so much more, impossibly more, attractive somehow.

'Well, I guess it wouldn't take long if you've already made it,' she heard herself say.

He gave her a crooked smile that clutched at her heart. 'Fine. Go on into the study and I'll bring you a cup.' He turned and headed for the kitchen.

Go now, she tried to tell herself, while he's out of the room. Don't stay with him alone. Don't tempt a situation you can't handle. But running wasn't going to help. She had to work with him on a tour in a few short weeks. She had to take hold of herself, get things into perspective.

Yvie walked slowly into the study. It still looked the same, apart from the addition of Josh's typewriter, the stack of paper, the crumpled sheets in the wastepaper bin and on the floor. Unconsciously she crossed to collect up the screwed up balls of paper that had missed the bin, tossing them in with the others.

'I'm afraid I couldn't quite get things to go right tonight,' he said from behind her and she spun around to face him.

'If you've been working on it all day perhaps you should have taken a break tonight,' she said uneasily.

'Perhaps.' He walked towards her and handed her a coffee mug.

They sipped the hot drink in silence. Yvie's coffee was just right. Milky, with no sugar. He'd remembered. Her eyes rose above the rim of her mug to find him looking at her, a strangely guarded expression in his eyes. Yvie looked away, her eyes settling on the pile of type-written pages.

'By the look of that you must be almost finished,' she said quickly because she had to say something to waylay the mounting tension silence was breeding.

'Three or four chapters should do it,' he replied offhandedly. 'I've a rough draft of all but the last one.'

'Dan will be pleased.' She glanced at him, hoping he wouldn't misconstrue her words as he had last time but he simply nodded.

'Mmm. And talking about Dan, I'd like to see him tomorrow. Any chance of a lift into the city in the morning?' he asked.

'I'll be leaving early,' Yvie began to put him off.

'That's all right. We can do a bit of shopping first thing. I've booked Tim and I on a tour after lunch. I promised Tim if he knuckled down with his studies we'd take a day off here and there to see something of the area. He's made a more than fair effort this week so I guess I'll have to keep my word.' He grimaced. 'Not that I'm terribly enthusiastic about a guided tour but,' he shrugged, 'we won't have the time to explore off our own bat.'

'You should enjoy it. I took a tour myself when I first arrived. San Francisco's an attractive city. I think so, anyway.' Yvie was relaxing a little.

'I suppose it's the impersonality of the tour that puts me off. It's so much more enjoyable to have someone who knows the area to show you around.'

'Yes, I guess it is,' Yvie agreed wondering if he was looking for her to offer to show them the highlights of the city. 'Dan took me on something of a sightseeing tour when I first arrived and some friends from work helped me find my way around.'

Josh's eyes fell broodingly to his coffee cup. 'And what does your husband think about you having,' he paused slightly, 'friends from work?'

His tone turned the words into an insult and Yvie could only stare at him wondering at his change of mood. She had been beginning to relax and now that same heightened tension was growing between them again. He was just like a jungle cat, sleek and languorous but dangerous all the while.

'Why should he mind that?' she asked levelly.

Josh shrugged.

'I have quite a number of friends at the office, after all, I've been here for two years.' Yvie could feel her anger rising at his cool cynical expression.

'That fellow who called looking for you today, Paul Rosetti, he seemed to be on more than friendly terms with you.'

Yvie's eyes widened incredulously. 'That's ridiculous! Paul's just a good friend.'

'And will you be telling your husband that you went out with this good friend?'

Yvie set her half empty coffee mug carefully on the table. 'I think I'll be going.' She advanced on him, her chin unconsciously set, determined to step self-possessedly around him.

His hand shot out to clasp her arm, stay her escape, fingers biting into her flesh.

'Take your hands off me!' she ordered, her voice heavy with disdain.

'Yvie, don't push me too far.' The warning came through his teeth.

'Or you'll what?' Yvie brushed his hand away. 'Look, Josh, if we're going to be able to work together then I'd appreciate it if you didn't try to maul me every time I come near you.'

He looked at her as though she'd mouthed a profanity and Yvie cringed inwardly with remorse. She was turning into a prize bitch and she couldn't like herself for it, nor could she stop herself. Josh brought out the worst in her, it seemed, although he never used to.

They stood glaring at each other and Josh was the first to move, turning away, hands once again on hips, his back stiff and taut.

'Goodnight, Yvie,' he said flatly and she watched an almost physical wave of tiredness wash over him.

How she longed to reach out and touch the smoothness of his back, massage away the tension, slide her fingers around over his flat stomach.

'Josh, perhaps I shouldn't have said that,' she began tightly. 'But surely you can see we can't go on like this.'

He turned slowly and sat back against the edge of the desk, arms folded across his chest.

'I mean, we have to work together and I'd, well, I'd rather we keep our relationship on a strictly business level. It's the only way we'll be able to get along.'

Her gaze rose to meet his and his eyes were mere slits, bright behind half closed lids, his expression cold and closed. He was silent for immeasurable seconds before he commented.

'You've changed, Yvie,' he said coolly. 'There was a time when you used to beg me to make love to you.'

Yvie blanched and then blushed fiery red.

'What's the matter, Yvie? Nothing to say? You've got a short memory. Or did you bundle up those particular memories like old love letters and bury them?'

Yvie flinched.

Pushing himself away from the desk Josh prowled closer to her, poised a body's width away from her. 'Well, Yvie? It was the truth, wasn't it?'

She drew herself together with no little effort. 'Josh, it was four years ago,' she began huskily.

'And I only have to touch you and those four years fade away to nothing.'

His voice was liquid silk and played its own hypnotising tune on her nerve endings. He lifted his hand, his fingers running sensuously along the length of her bare arm and Yvie shivered involuntarily. His thumb found the pulse beating at the base of her throat and lingered caressingly there. Yvie closed her eyes, her mouth going dry as a flood of longing rose within her.

'Josh, please, don't do this to me.'

'Don't do it?' He laughed brokenly. 'I can no more stop touching you than I can cease breathing,' he said and his lips replaced his thumb, his hands pulling her slowly against him.

If he'd been forceful or demanding then perhaps she would have fought him off, pushed him from her. But his lips were gentle, almost reverent, and before his mouth found hers she was lost to him. Her body arched against his, her hands going around him, her fingers playing over his firm muscular back.

She was enfolded in him, absorbed, and her hands slid upwards, her fingers twining now in his soft fair hair the way they used to do. Josh's lips left her mouth to tease her earlobe and Yvie murmured impassionedly, her body moving against his, aflame for him.

Josh's breathing was ragged and she knew he was fast losing control. Leaning back from her, his hands framed her face, the pad of one thumb brushing gently against her lips, tantalising her, and she trembled in his hold.

Josh drew in a deep breath, his heartbeats beneath her hands resting on his chest racing as though he'd been running. He closed his eyes and when he opened them they were blue-black and the lines on either side of his mouth were deeply etched.

'God, Yvie, can you deny how it is with us? Can you tell me now that it's over?'

She couldn't find her voice to reply, and she was unable to drag her gaze from his. He held her eyes with the fire of passion blazing in his.

'Or is it the same with any man, with that guy this afternoon, with your husband?' His lips twisted cruelly and his fingers tightened, bruising her.

His words sank through Yvie's mist of euphoria and she came back to earth with a thud. Her rush of anger gave her a burst of strength to snatch his hands away and she stumbled back from him.

'How could you?' she demanded of him. 'How can you be such a bloody hypocrite? You think you can push me out of your life until it's convenient for you to pick me up again and . . . and . . .' Yvie drew an infuriated breath. 'What makes you think I'd spend the time waiting around for you?'

'You hardly did that, did you?' he remarked sarcastically. 'You married someone else pretty damn quickly,' he bit out.

Yvie was far too angry for tears and the pain inside her stabbed mercilessly, finding its way relentlessly to the deepest, most brutal hurt of all.

'That rankles, doesn't it, Josh? That I could marry someone else? That I could forget the great Josh Graham? Well, I did. And my one regret is that I ever met you, that I allowed you to touch me. I should have stayed with Larry instead of being blinded by your glib lies, because Larry's good and kind and he married me even knowing——' Yvie's voice caught in her throat and tears now filled her eyes. 'Larry's twice the person you'll ever be, Josh Graham.'

He took a step towards her but she held up her hand and shook her head.

'No! Don't!' She bit her lip to still its tremble. 'And you know something else? I wish you'd kept out of my life, that I never had to see you again.' Her voice caught on a sob. 'You haven't changed, Josh. You're still the same selfish person you always were, using people and then discarding them when it suits you. You have no more integrity than you had four years ago. And I'm not going to let you start it all over again. I'm not!'

Without giving him time to say a word she spun on her heel and ran out of the study and down the hallway, tripped down the stairs, not stopping until the door of her flat was locked securely behind her.

The tears came then, in a deluge, and she sank on to the sofa, burying her face in a soft cushion. She cried as she hadn't cried since she made her new life here in San Francisco. The two years before that had been all tears. Now she was weeping again for the past. She hadn't, after all, left so very far behind.

She wept for everything she'd lost; for the Josh Graham she'd loved and what they'd had together; for her father whose heart she'd almost broken; for Larry, who had had the capacity to forgive her; and for her daughter, hers and Josh's, who had struggled to be born and fought hard for life and lost the battle.

By the time her sobs had subsided Yvie felt tired, strained and totally drained, drained of all emotion. She'd thought she'd never cry over it all again. She'd told herself she wouldn't allow anything or anybody to rake it all up once more. But she'd reckoned without Josh Graham. It was all his doing.

If he'd stayed in the past all this would never have happened. She'd have gone on with her life, with some measure of inner tranquillity and left those unhappy years behind her for this had been her fresh start. And she'd succeeded. In these two years she had sorted herself out, pulled her life together. And now Josh Graham had put paid to all that, had undone all her careful reconstruction.

Eventually she undressed and crawled into bed. How she wished desperately that she could shut it all out by simply closing her eyes. But darkness only brought her memories swirling forward in a huge deluge.

It seemed her tears had washed away all the carefully placed covers she'd banked over her deepest recollections, baring them, bringing them back with absolute clarity. She could almost experience again the quickening she'd felt inside her when the doctor had confirmed her pregnancy. And she knew again the tumult of emotions that had churned about within her.

Josh was away at the time, on one of his semi-regular trips down to Brisbane, and a couple of months had passed since their first night together, the first of many wonderfully ecstatic nights of shared passion, of self and mutual discovery. When she returned from her visit to the doctor Yvie had sat on the beach alone, watching the sea beat upon the sand, for once not really seeing it.

She frowned faintly. Josh had seemed strained somehow when he'd called to say goodbye. There were lines of stress around his mouth that had momentarily disappeared when he smiled at her, but now that she gave it some thought in retrospect his smile hadn't quite reached his eyes.

He wasn't sure how long he'd be away this time, he'd said, but he'd be back as soon as he could. He had to get on with his book which was almost half completed. But the tension had been there, she was sure of it.

Until now Yvie hadn't given it a thought. Her thoughts had been entirely taken up with the idea that she may be pregnant. Now she knew she was. Deep down inside her part of Josh and part of herself was growing, the result of their love.

And she'd alternated between delight and disquiet. She was worried about how her father would take the news. He was very old fashioned about things like that, believed in a staunch moral code. But when she married Josh it would be fine. He would be as pleased as she was about the baby, his grandchild.

She was absolutely thrilled herself and she knew Josh would be, too. After all, he loved her. They loved each other. They would be married and then they could be together all the time.

At this point her daydreams faltered fleetingly. Josh had never actually said he loved her, not in words, but his body had told her every time he touched her. Of course he loved her, as she loved him. For ever. Irrevocably. And he'd be as rapt about the baby as she was.

She hugged herself excitedly wondering for the first time if she would have a girl or a boy. He or she would be fair as they both were, and maybe with Josh's blue eyes.

Only when she was with her father did some of her excitement dim. He was still far from well and she hoped her news wouldn't upset him. The thought of telling him filled her with apprehension.

A whole week passed before Josh returned. And he hadn't called over to their cottage straight away, as he usually did. Yvie wouldn't have known he was back if she hadn't gone for a solitary walk along the beach after dinner. She was drawn as far along as Josh's unit, wanting to be with him, close to him. And his light was burning. She knew instinctively that the light was his.

Her bare feet grew wings as she ran across the loose dry sand, not noticing the pull on the muscles of her legs as her feet squeaked in the sand's softness. Inside, the elevator purred silently upwards, the doors gliding open on the eighth floor.

Yvie walked across the carpeted floor to the door of his unit, her heart beating excitedly. She would be seeing him again and she would tell him about the baby and they would make plans. She pressed the bell and waited.

Josh was some time answering her ring and when he finally opened the door she was taken aback by his appearance. His face looked grey and pinched with tiredness and his eyes were red rimmed and bloodshot.

'Hi!' She greeted him softly, wanting to wrap her arms about him, let him lean against her. But something held her back. 'I saw your light on so I came up. I ... wanted to see you, to tell you something.'

He wiped his hand across his eyes and his shoulders seemed to slump.

'Yvie, you'd better come in,' he said at last and stood back for her to enter.

Her smile fading, Yvie walked inside and stood watching him a little warily. What could be wrong? He hadn't even kissed her. In fact, she could have sworn he hadn't even wanted her there.

'What did you want to tell me?' he asked flatly.

'Josh, what's the matter?' Her stomach was tightening nervously.

He sighed deeply and raked his fair hair with his fingers.

'Did you have a bad trip?' she asked quietly, her eyes drinking in his drawn features.

'You could say that.' His tone was flat, expressionless. 'Yvie, I——' He seemed to be having trouble deciding what to say and he rubbed his temples as though his head ached.

Yvie crossed to him, covered one of his hands with her own. 'Josh, what is it? Aren't you feeling well?' She was becoming more concerned by the minute.

'No, I'm fine. Just tired,' he replied and his eyes rose to meet hers. He flinched slightly. 'Yvie, I——' He shook his head and reached blindly for her, folding her in his arms, holding her tightly to him.

He stood like that for an eternity, not speaking, and Yvie was just happy to be close to him, feel the security of his arms about her. His lips moved against her forehead and then he gently put her from him, sat her down, and seated himself opposite her.

'Yvie, I have to talk to you.'

'What about?' She raised her eyes innocently towards him and his eyes fell.

'About us. About me. And I don't know where to start.'

'Josh?' Yvie felt her heart beginning to sink. Something was dreadfully wrong. But what?

'I have to go away,' he said at last.

'Away?' She mouthed the word and swallowed. 'Where to?'

'To Brisbane first. And then to England.'

'England?' Yvie repeated incredulously. Her throat constricted and she swallowed again. 'How . . . how long will you be gone?' she breathed the question, although deep inside she felt his answer.

Josh shrugged, his eyes not meeting hers. 'At this stage I don't know.'

Silence stretched uncomfortably between them.

'Can I come, too?' she asked before she could draw back the words and she flushed bright red at her presumption. How could she have asked that? Where was her pride?

Josh leant backwards against the chair, his eyes on the ceiling. 'I wish——' He took a deep breath. 'How I wish it was that simple.' He sat forward again, his elbows resting lightly on his knees. 'Yvie, I haven't been totally honest with you, God help me.'

Yvie couldn't speak. She sat stiffly watching him, mesmerised.

'But please believe I did, I do, love you. More than I can tell you.' His hand reached out to touch her and then fell back, his eyes filled with an inner agony she couldn't understand.

'Josh, what is it?' Yvie was numb all over and her head swam alarmingly.

Josh's lips twisted. 'The truth of it, Yvie, is that I haven't had the right to love you, to make love to you, no matter now much I've wanted to.' He stopped and looked burningly into her eyes. 'And you know how much I've wanted to make love to you.'

He stood up and walked restlessly around the room. 'I thought in the beginning that I would be able to work it out but now I know I can't. I was a blind fool to think I ever could,' he finished self-derisively.

A cold stab of fear seared through the numbness clutching at every one of Yvie's sensitised nerve endings. He was trying to tell her it was all over between them.

Slowly she stood up, her eyes locked on the tall familiarity of him. She was unconsciously taking in every facet of him, every intimate feature, committing it to memory. The way his hair curled over the collar of his shirt, the hard breadth of his shoulders, the taper to narrow waist and hips, his long muscular legs. She could almost feel the remembered texture of his skin beneath her questing fingertips, the way his body quivered to her touch as they lay together. And the rightness of that coming together.

How could he mean it was all over? That their . . . Their what? Their affair! Yvie cringed. Was that what they had had? An affair that was now over?

'Yvie, we can't see each other any more,' he said quietly, not looking at her, and when she said nothing he slowly turned. 'Yvie, believe me, this isn't the way I meant it to be. It's the way it has to be.' His voice was raw, as though it caught in his throat.

Yvie was completely numb now. It was only later that the pain began.

'Why, Josh?' she asked through lips stiff and cold.

Josh raised his hands and let them fall. 'Because,' he paused, 'because I'm not free to love you, to——' He stopped and closed his eyes mementarily. 'Yvie, I'm already married. I have a wife.' He said the word as though it was unfamiliar to him.

CHAPTER EIGHT

'A WIFE?' Yvie folded her arms about herself in a primitive form of protection.

'Yes. She . . . Renee and I have been married for nine years. On and off,' he added bitterly.

Yvie stared at him, white-faced. She really felt quite faint and she began to draw in deep steadying breaths.

'When I met you,' Josh continued, 'and fell in love with you I attempted to ask Renee for a divorce, there was little left of our marriage, God knows. But she's fought me all the way. She has the trump card and she damn well knows it.'

He ran his hand through his hair again. 'So it's a stalemate.'

'Are you . . . do you love her?' Yvie asked chokedly.

'I did. Briefly. But by the time I realised I'd made a mistake it was too late.' He rubbed his jaw with his hand. 'Now she has our son and if I sue her for a divorce she's going to fight for custody. She's not,' he drew a breath, 'I can't let her have free rein with him, Yvie. He's my son and I'm responsible for him.'

He walked across to the bar and splashed whiskey into a glass, downing it straight. 'I had word that my mother-in-law was taken ill. She's not expected to live and I have to go back.'

Setting down the empty glass he turned back

towards her, keeping space between them. Yvie, understand that I didn't want things to end between us. I've never wanted anything more in my life, but,' he paused.

'But you have a wife and a son,' Yvie found her voice and finished for him. 'And you have to go back to them.'

'Yvie.' He crossed to her then, went to pull her into his arms, but she backed away from him, shaking her head.

'No, Josh. Don't touch me.'

'Yvie, try to understand. I love you.' His face was drawn and haggard.

'Josh, please! No more. No more lies. Just go back to your wife.'

Turning on her heel she ran out of the unit. She didn't even attempt to wait for the elevator but thrust open the door to the stairs and raced downwards as though the devil himself was on her heels. But she needn't have worried, for Josh didn't even attempt to follow her, and she reached the cottage before she slowed her pace.

Luckily her father was in bed when she arrived home for she must have looked a sight, hair tangled from the wind, tears gushing down her cheeks, and she fell on to her bed, alone in her misery. She had never felt so wretched in her life.

When she awoke the bedroom swam and she just made it to the bathroom before she was violently ill. Her father was full of concern and wanted to call their doctor but she assured him it was simply something she'd eaten, that she'd feel better if she lay down, spent the morning in bed.

He hovered worriedly over her making her feel even more guilty and ill.

Finally she drifted off to sleep and didn't stir until lunchtime. She sat up slowly and walked gingerly into the kitchen. Her father was sitting at the kitchen table reading his newspaper.

'Feeling better, love?' he asked sympathetically.

'Much better. I think I'll make some tea.' She avoided meeting his eyes. 'Would you like a cup?'

'Love one,' he smiled.

They had just sat down when Josh arrived. He'd come to say goodbye. His mother-in-law had taken ill, he told Jim Matthews, his eyes glancing quickly at Yvie.

She sat clutching her tea cup and the pain that had racked her body the night before began again, achingly. Josh shook hands with her father and Yvie steeled herself. She raised her eyes to meet his, to hold his gaze.

'Goodbye, Josh,' she said evenly, although it cost her dearly.

His lips tightened and his eyelids fell to shutter the bleakness in his eyes. 'Goodbye, Yvie,' he said and he was gone.

'We'll miss Josh calling in, won't we?' remarked her father as he stood by the door watching the car pull away. 'I seem to think I heard somewhere that his wasn't a happy marriage,' Jim reflected. 'I don't recall him mentioning his wife, do you?'

Yvie shook her head.

'Still, could have been gossip. You know how people love to talk.' He picked up his tea cup.

Morning sickness hit Yvie heavily and she realised her abject depression couldn't be helping. As much as she tried to keep it from her father he was bound to notice her constant paleness and tiredness.

'Yvie, this isn't like you,' he said worriedly a week later. 'I insist you see the doctor. It could be something serious.'

Yvie looked up at him and burst into tears. 'Oh, Dad. Dad. I don't need to see a doctor. I know what's wrong with me. I'm ... I'm pregnant,' she finished quickly before she lost her nerve to tell him.

Jim Matthews sat down suddenly, his face white with shock. Yvie hurried to him.

'Dad, are you all right? I didn't mean to blurt it out like that but I——' She dissolved into tears again.

Her father was silent for some seconds and then he seemed to drag himself together. 'Now, now. Stop crying, love, you'll only make yourself worse.'

Yvie wiped her face with her hands. 'Oh, Dad, I'm sorry. I didn't mean to do this to you. I——' She knelt down beside his chair and he lifted a trembling hand to brush back her hair.

'How long have you known?'

'Not long. About a week,' she replied. 'Dad, I'll go away and——'

'Now we'll have none of that. You'll stay here where you belong,' he told her firmly. 'I suppose it's young Larry. Have you told him yet?'

Yvie gazed incredulously up at her father. He thought it was Larry. He didn't know, hadn't guessed about her and Josh. But Larry had only been up to the coast twice in the past few months, and only once since Josh had come to stay.

And she'd been on tenterhooks for the two days Larry had stayed with them because she couldn't be with Josh. When Larry went back to his ship Josh had teased her, asked her if he had a rival? She hastened to reassure him, kissed him, and they'd made love.

'You'll have to tell him, Yvie,' her father was saying. 'He has a right to know. Do you want to marry him?'

'Marry him?' Yvie repeated stupidly.

'When he finds out I'm sure Larry will want to do the right thing. The baby's his, when all's said and done. I'll speak to him.' Her father nodded determinedly.

Larry the father of her baby. Yvie almost laughed hysterically. Why, she and Larry had never progressed past affectionate kisses although Larry—Yvie stopped. Larry had indicated he wanted more than friendship between them, but by then Josh was here and she hadn't seen anyone else.

'Dad, please, I'm not sure I want, well, I'd rather you didn't say anything. It . . . it should come from me and, well,' Yvie gulped guiltily. She was deliberately misleading her father.

Jim patted her hand. 'I understand. But I think you should write to him.'

Of course she didn't write to Larry. She couldn't. It was nothing to do with him. And she knew she'd have to tell her father the truth but each time she tried to broach the subject she couldn't quite manage to bring herself to do it. To find out that it was Josh Graham she was involved with might be too much for her father to take. He held Josh in such high esteem and she was loath to crush her father's illusions the way Josh had shattered hers. While she procrastinated fate stepped in and set the course of her life.

She was on the beach when Larry arrived, unannounced, so her father was the first to speak to him. Larry was on special leave for two weeks and as his parents were overseas he had called up to see Yvie and her father.

When he came out on to the beach and sat down beside her Yvie felt herself go pale.

'Larry. What are you doing here?' she asked breathily.

'Came to see my girl.' He smiled, although the smile didn't quite reach his eyes.

Yvie could tell he knew and her gaze fell. She couldn't find her voice to say a word.

'I've been talking to your father,' he said, confirming her worst imaginings.

'Larry, I——'

He held up his hand. 'I told him I did want to marry you.' His eyes held hers. 'And I meant every word of it, Yvie.'

She could only gaze up at him and then a rush of tears welled in her eyes. 'Oh, Larry, I'm so sorry. I didn't mean for Dad to get the wrong idea. He just surmised that you . . . that you were the one and I couldn't bring myself to tell him otherwise at the time. But I was going to tell him, please believe me. I just didn't expect you to come home so soon.'

Tears trickled down her cheeks and she dashed them away with the back of her hand. She seemed to do nothing more than cry these days.

'Don't cry, Yvie.' Larry put his arm around her and she turned into his shoulder.

'Oh, Larry, I'm so ashamed of myself getting you entangled in this mess.'

'Want to tell me about it?' he asked gently.

'There's not much to tell. I was simply a mammoth fool and made the biggest mistake of my life. Now I guess I'll have to live with it,' she finished flatly.

'He, the guy, he doesn't want to marry you?'

Yvie shook her head. 'No. He couldn't if he wanted to, which he doesn't. He's already married with a family.' She raised her eyes to his. 'But I didn't know that until it was too late.'

And would it have made any difference if she had known about his wife. She liked to think it would but . . . she'd never know.

'Yvie, I meant what I said,' Larry repeated. 'I do want to marry you. You know how I've always felt about you.'

Yvie shook her head emphatically. 'No, Larry. I can't let you even contemplate it. Not that I don't appreciate it. You don't know how much I do, but no, I can't let you do it.'

'You can't stop me wanting to marry you, Yvie,' he said firmly. 'And I don't want you going through it all alone. If it's humanly possible a kid needs two parents and you have my word I'll be as good a father to the baby as if it were my own.'

'Oh, Larry, don't! You make me feel so, so selfish.' Yvie covered her face with her hands.

'It would be for the best, Yvie. Can't you see that? I love you.'

'That's just it, Larry. I don't want to hurt you. You don't deserve that. But I don't love you the same way. I like you, I even love you, but as a brother, the brother I always wanted and never had.'

'Marriages have started out on less than that,' he told her seriously. 'And I'm willing to take the chance that you'll learn to love me, too.'

Yvie hesitated and then shook her head. 'I couldn't. It's not fair on you, Larry.'

'I should be the judge of that. I want to marry you, Yvie. I'm not being forced into it. Your father hasn't been holding a gun to my head. It's my own decision.' He lifted her chin so that she was looking at him. 'I was hoping we'd make a go of it anyway, get married eventually. This just brings it forward.'

'But Larry, I'm having another man's child,' Yvie began.

'It's your child, too, and if the father doesn't want to face up to his responsibilities then he forfeits the right as I see it. I love you, Yvie, and I couldn't help but love any part of you.'

Yvie could only gaze up at him and he wrapped his arms around her and held her. She let out a tired sigh. It was so nice to lean on someone after shouldering alone the burden of what to do. And the burden had been getting harder to bear each day.

'Do I take your silence as an acceptance of my proposal?' he asked softly against her hair.

Yvie looked up at him and nodded reluctantly.

Larry's lips lifted in his boyish grin. 'Great!'

He kissed her gently, his mouth firm and pleasant on hers but she drew away. Not that his kisses repelled her, but they reminded her of Josh and what they'd shared together and lost.

'You haven't asked who he was. Don't you want to know?' she asked him.

'Not particularly. But I think I can guess,' he added evenly.

Yvie's eyes widened in surprise.

'The writer fellow who was here last time I was on leave. Josh something-or-other.'

'Josh Graham.' It even hurt to say his name. 'How did you know?'

Larry shrugged. 'I sensed the change in you and I saw the way you looked at him, something like the way I look at you. I just had to hope you'd get him out of your system and remember me.'

'Oh, Larry. I'm sorry,' she whispered.

'Why?' he gave her a quick squeeze. 'It's his loss and I got you in the end, didn't I?'

So she married Larry. Because he was there and she needed someone. The marriage had been doomed from the start and it didn't take Yvie long to realise it.

They had only had one night together before Larry rejoined his ship and Yvie could still shudder over that night. It had been a total disaster and it was all her fault. How she wished she could have been in love with Larry, that Josh Graham had never come into her life. Perhaps then their marriage may have had a chance of succeeding.

Larry had deserved so much and she had given so little. When Larry kissed her Josh's image had come between them, when Larry tried to make love to her she simply froze.

Poor Larry. He'd assured her that everything would be all right once the baby was born and he kept on telling her that the few times he had leave over the next couple of months.

In actual fact her life went on much the same as it had done before she'd met Josh. She lived in the cottage with her father and Larry came home every so often. If her father noticed their constraint, that they slept in separate bedrooms he made no comment. Yvie simply drifted, and even the impending arrival of her baby didn't seem to be totally real.

Larry was at sea when the baby decided to arrive early. Yvie's delivery was long and difficult and developed complications that ended in a hurried Caesarean. Yvie's daughter lived for a few hours and Yvie returned to the cottage feeling more alone than she'd ever felt in her life. The doctor assured her she could have other children but she knew she wouldn't.

When Yvie lost the baby Larry flew home but kind as he was he couldn't console her. She knew their marriage wasn't going to work but when she suggested a divorce Larry wouldn't hear of it. They would work it out.

To make matters worse Yvie's father's health had deteriorated and, by the time Josh's book appeared to take the literary world by storm, he was confined to his bed. Yvie nursed him to the end and a week after his death one of his associates offered her a position in a small publishing firm.

Yvie threw herself into her job with a will, for while she worked she could shut out everything else. It was only at night that despair took over and her tears fell. She lost weight, fined down, her face going from teenage fullness to a reserved beauty. And sadness shadowed her grey eyes.

A year after she started with the publishing company, having more than proved herself capable and competent, she was given the chance to go to San Francisco and work with Dan Kirkoff. It was a heaven sent opportunity for she'd grown restless, knowing she had to shake herself out of her hollow introverted existence.

Her divorce from Larry, a mutual decision to end their marriage that hadn't even begun, had been finalised a few months earlier so there was nothing to keep her in Australia. She and Larry had parted friends although she knew he felt their break-up far more than she did.

She could see that their lack of a physical relationship was getting to Larry and she knew for his sake she had to make a clean break or make their marriage into a real one. She couldn't bring herself to take the latter step for her memories of Josh were always there to remind her of how it should have been. If she settled for less she would not only be cheating Larry but she'd be cheating herself. As much as she wanted to she could never feel about Larry the way she'd felt about Josh.

She had finally persuaded Larry that there was no future in their staying together. He had taken some convincing, but she knew she had to do it, if only for his sake. He deserved another chance, the chance of meeting someone who would make him happy.

At least it assuaged some of her guilt. She'd married Larry for her own selfish reasons and she'd used him as a shield ever since. She wanted no more close relationships and when someone came too near or showed an interest in her she flashed her wedding ring as a deterrent. She had used Larry all along and she couldn't forgive herself for that.

And so she'd left her old life behind and moved to San Francisco. She settled in to her job and met and made new friends. It was all working out perfectly. Until Josh Graham reappeared and drove her back into the past with unrelenting ease.

Next morning Yvie used more makeup than she was wont to use for there were dark circles under her eyes and her face looked pale and wan. She touched some blush to her cheeks and when she was satisfied with the results she climbed into her light grey skirt and slipped on a pale blue shirt. The collar buttoned to the neck and the sleeves were full with wide fitted cuffs. A matching grey waistcoat went with the outfit, but after glancing at her wristwatch and noticing the time she slung the waistcoat over her arm, grabbed her handbag, and hurried through to the garage.

She was pulled up short at the sight of Josh and Tim leaning against the bonnet of her car. Josh had wanted a lift into the office. Of course. How could she have forgotten?

'Hi Yvie! We were beginning to think you'd slept in,' Tim grinned. He was dressed in jeans and sneakers and his iridescent sweat shirt and he had a sweater tied by the sleeves around his shoulders.

'No, I didn't sleep in.' Didn't sleep was more like it, she added to herself. 'I'm just running a little late, that's all.'

Her eyes glanced over Josh and slid away. He wore a grey three piece suit, a shade darker than her own suit, with a pale blue shirt and contrasting tie. The colours suited his blond hair and tanned skin and Yvie couldn't deny that he was by far the most attractive man she'd ever known.

He pushed himself away from the car and walked around to open the car door for her. Their eyes clashed again as she slid around him and she couldn't exhale the breath she was holding until he'd closed the door and turned to walk around to the passenger side. She was unaware of the worried frown on Tim's face as his gaze went from the closed quietness of his father to Yvie's unsmiling face.

The evening before hung heavily between them and while Josh settled himself in the car Yvie busied herself adjusting her seatbelt and fitting the key into the ignition. Anything to keep from acknowledging her body's explosive reaction to his nearness.

The drive into the city was a relatively silent one with only Tim attempting to keep up a flow of conversation and it wasn't long before even he gave up.

'Is there somewhere near here where I can get my film developed?' he asked her as they climbed out of the car in the parking area beneath the building that housed the offices of Dan's publishing company.

'I think there's a fast film developing service in the mall on the first floor.' Yvie glanced at her watch again. 'Would you like to drop it off on the way up?'

'Could we? I want to see how the photos I took at dinner the other night came out. And the ones I took in the plane coming here.'

'It won't make you late, will it?' Josh asked joining in the conversation for the first time.

Yvie gave a soft laugh. 'I'm already late so a few minutes more is neither here nor there.'

They got off at the first floor and attended to Tim's film and then reentered the elevator.

'I'll take you straight in to Dan's office.' Yvie told the knot of Josh's tie as the lift sped upwards.

'Fine.' Josh replied, equally distantly.

The first person they ran into was Abby. She was hurrying out of the typists' office and stopped mid stride, her face a picture of total surprise.

'Morning, Yvie,' she smiled, recovering quickly, her dark eyes alive with interest going to Josh.

'Hello, Abby.' Yvie had to stop and make the introductions.

Abby held out her hand and Josh took it, a smile lighting his face.

'Please to meet you, Josh,' Abby purred and

Yvie couldn't really blame her, anyone would when Josh turned on the charm. 'We've heard so much about you, and read your marvellous books.'

'Thank you.' Josh was still smiling and seemed to let Abby's hand go with reluctance.

Yvie watched him from beneath her lashes and her heart turned over painfully. He used to smile at her like that once. She pulled herself up short. If Josh Graham wanted to smile at Abby, who cared? Not Yvie, that was sure.

She realised the tapping of typewriters had stopped and the typists were all agog, eyes on Josh. Really! You'd think they'd never seen a man before, Yvie frowned, and there were plenty who were as attractive as Josh Graham.

'Is Dan in his office?' she asked Abby a little sharply and Abby raised her eyebrows at her tone.

'Sure is,' she said, her eyes questioning Yvie.

'We'd better get along then,' Yvie said, not looking at her friend. Good grief! Now she'd upset Abby. Was this going to continue all the time Josh was here? She'd be a raving neurotic before then if she didn't get herself together.

'Okay. See you around, Josh,' Abby smiled again. ' 'Bye, Tim.'

Yvie hoped they didn't run into anyone else. She just wanted to deposit Josh and run. With a small sigh of relief she tapped on Dan's door and stepped inside.

'Good morning, Dan.'

Dan glanced up from his desk, glasses on the end of his nose. 'Hi, Yvie.' He caught sight of

Josh behind her and stood up beaming, throwing his glasses on the desk and lumbering around with hand outstretched. 'Josh. Good to see you.' He pumped Josh's hand. 'And how are you, young fellow?'

'Fine, thanks,' replied Tim.

'Well, I'll leave you to it,' put in Yvie. 'I'll be in my office,' she told Dan, and with a quick smile for Tim she hurried outside, not looking to right or left until she reached the sanctuary of her office. She sank into her chair and resting her elbows on the desk gently massaged her temples with her fingertips.

'Yvie!' Her door burst open. 'Oh, sorry. Got a headache?' asked Abby sympathetically.

'Just a dull one,' she replied straightening in her chair. 'If I stop thinking about it it will go away.'

'You should take something for it before it gets any worse.'

'Mmm,' Yvie murmured and prepared herself for the reason for Abby's visit. Who else would be the topic of conversation but Josh Graham.

'Paul gave me these for you to go through.' Abby produced a sheaf of papers. 'Anytime before Friday, he said.'

'Oh. Right. Thanks.' Yvie took the papers a little sheepishly.

Abby chuckled. 'Shame on you, Yvie. You thought I came in for an avid gossip about Josh Graham, didn't you?'

Yvie laughed softly and nodded.

Grabbing a chair Abby sat down opposite Yvie. 'Well, I did. The papers were just an excuse. Oh, Yvie, he's divine.'

'Divine?' Yvie half laughed, although the sound stuck in her throat.

'One of the typist's descriptions,' grimaced Abby. 'But she's not far wrong. He's the most attractive guy I've seen in ages.'

'He's all right,' Yvie said flatly.

'All right? Are you out of your tiny mind, Yvie Dean? Or are you not seeing things too clearly these days?'

'Oh, Abby, there are plenty of good looking men around. He's just one of many.'

'Where are they, just tell me that?' Abby raised her hands and let them fall.

'Take Paul, for instance. He's attractive, too.'

'If you like dark sultry types,' said Abby drily.

'Which you do,' Yvie reminded her. She knew Abby would have jumped at the chance of going out with Paul if she hadn't been working with him. Abby also didn't like to mix business with pleasure.

'Okay. So Paul Rosetti's attractive, too. But today's the day for tanned and rugged blonds.' She sighed heavily and Yvie couldn't prevent herself from laughing.

'Oh, Abby, you're the limit.'

'Maybe, but you're the lucky one, living with him and all.'

Yvie flushed. 'I'd hardly call it living with him, Abby. We rarely see each other.' Her eyes fell and she nervously shuffled her papers. And when we do see each other we either fight or——'

'Gee! What a waste!' Abby grimaced exaggeratedly. 'I'd be running out of everything. Any excuse and I'd be up there. And his son's going to grow up just like him by the look of him.'

'Yes. Tim's a nice boy.' Yvie felt on safer ground. 'Josh's taking him on a tour this afternoon. He'd like to get out to see Yosemite, too, but Josh doesn't think he'll have time to take him.'

'I think Paul's father's taking his young brothers out camping to Yosemite. Why not see if you can arrange for Tim to go with them. I think he said they were going this weekend.'

Yvie frowned. 'It would be a great opportunity for Tim to see the Park, but perhaps Mr Rosetti might think three boys of his own are enough to handle.'

'No harm in asking,' shrugged Abby.

'Mmm. I'll talk to Paul about it this afternoon.'

'Did I hear my name mentioned?' Paul stuck his head around the door and strolled in to perch himself on the edge of Yvie's desk. 'Are you girls trying to decide which one of you will come out with me next?'

Abby gave a deprecatory snort. Yvie chuckled and explained about Tim and Yosemite.

'Dad would be pleased to take him along and young Angelo's about his age. They'd think it was great having an English boy to show around.'

'Then perhaps you could ask your father if he's willing to take Tim before I broach the subject with Josh. I know Tim's really keen to see the Park.'

'I'll phone Dad this afternoon.' Paul leaned over and cupped Yvie's cheek with his hand. 'Anything for you, honey lamb,' he drawled teasingly.

'So this is where you all are.' Dan walked into

the office followed by Josh and Tim. 'I was
beginning to think it was lunchtime.'

'Executive meeting, Dan.' Paul stood up and
smiled easily at his boss. 'We were discussing
matters of vital importance to the company.'

'I'm sure,' said Dan drily and began the
introductions. 'I'm taking Josh around to meet
everyone. You can come, too, Paul.'

'Right.' Paul turned back to Yvie and gave her
a broad wink. 'I'll get back to you later on that
other matter.' He shot a quick look at Tim and
Yvie nodded.

Her eyes were drawn of their own accord to
Josh and his face was set and expressionless and
he didn't look as though he was enjoying himself.

'Ah, Dad.' Tim spoke up as Josh went to leave
the office. 'Can I stay with Yvie while you meet
everyone? You won't be long and I'd rather stay
here.'

Josh looked across at Yvie. 'If it's all right with
Yvie.'

'Yes, of course. He can stay if he likes.' Yvie's
throat constricted as Tim grinned at her with
Josh's smile. Abby was right. In a few years'
time Tim would be every bit as attractive as his
father.

'I've brought a book.' He held up a paperback.
'So I won't disturb you.'

Dan, Josh and Paul left the office and Abby
stood up too. 'I'd better go and earn my money, I
suppose. See you both later.'

'You don't mind me staying here, do you,
Yvie?' Tim asked when they were alone.

'No, of course not.'

'That's good. I was a bit bored while Dad and Mr Kirkoff were talking. I don't think I'm ready for big business yet.' He sat down in the chair Abby had been sitting in and swung his legs over one arm. 'I'm reading a Hardy Boys mystery. It's not bad either,' he said as he flipped through the pages and began to fill her in on the story so far.

He stopped and grinned. 'I'm not letting you get your work done, am I?'

'No, you're not.' Yvie laughed and then noticed the sober expression on Tim's face.

'I like you, Yvie,' he said. 'I can talk to you.'

'Why, thank you, Tim. That's nice. And I like you, too.' Yvie was just a little taken aback.

'Have you been married long?' he asked just as Yvie began to read the top page.

She looked up. 'I was married four years ago.'

'Oh. That long. Why isn't your husband here with you?'

'Larry's in the Navy,' she replied carefully.

'The American Navy?'

'No, the Australian.'

'How often does he get to come to the States?'

Yvie hesitated. 'Not often,' she replied honestly, and Tim's eyes held hers. She sighed. 'We aren't together anymore. We were divorced two years ago.'

'Oh.' Tim let out a soft whistle and grinned from ear to ear. 'Oh,' he repeated and then sobered. 'Sorry, Yvie. I didn't mean to pry.'

'That's all right. I just don't talk about it much.' Why had she told Tim? she asked herself. If he told Josh—

'No, I guess you wouldn't.' Tim glanced down at his book and Yvie returned to her work.

'Yvie?' Tim spoke again. 'Do you like Dad?'

Her hands stilled as she sorted Paul's papers. 'Like him?' She felt herself tense. 'Yes, I like him. Why do you ask?'

Tim shrugged. 'I think he kind of likes you.'

Her heartbeats raced and then slowed. 'Now, Tim,' she began breathily.

'I know. It's none of my business and don't interfere. Dad told me that, too.'

'Your father told——' My God, what had he been saying to Josh? Yvie went hot all over.

Tim nodded. 'I told Dad I liked you. I just wanted him to know.'

'What did he say?' The words were out before she could stop them.

'Not much. He went all adult and frowned sort of vaguely. That's when he told me it was none of my business and not to interfere.'

'I see.' Yvie stood up. She had to do something. 'Would you like a cup of tea or coffee?' she asked him as she walked across to the small beverage heater on one of her filing cabinets.

'No, thanks.' She could feel him watching her as she poured hot water over her tea bag and lifted it out of the cup.

'Yvie?'

Good grief! What was coming now? She kept her back to him and made a chore of stirring her tea. 'Mmm?'

'What were you and Dad fighting about last night?'

Yvie almost dropped her cup. She turned slowly to face him. 'Fighting about?'

Tim nodded. 'I was in bed, but I wasn't asleep. I heard the raised voices and I knew it was you and Dad.'

'Well, I interrupted his writing,' she began, 'when I left my key in the house and had to ask your father to let me in.'

'Dad doesn't usually let that bother him.' Tim frowned.

'Maybe things weren't going too well with his book and he was tired.'

'Maybe.' Tim sighed. 'I kind of hoped you'd like Dad.'

'I told you I do like him,' she repeated feeling herself flush. 'Now don't go worrying about last night. I've already forgotten it.' Oh, Tim, if you only knew. 'Your father seems quite nice. I don't really know him that well.' Yvie stopped, swallowing quickly.

'He's a great guy, really he is,' Tim told her enthusiastically.

'I believe you. But Tim, you don't have to sell him to me. He's a very famous writer.' She half laughed. 'What's behind this anyway?'

'Well, I kind of hoped you two might get together.'

'Get together?' Yvie choked. 'But ... Tim, what about your mother?'

'Mum?' Tim shrugged. 'My mother died over a year ago.'

CHAPTER NINE

Yvie sat down heavily. 'She died? Oh, Tim, I'm sorry. I didn't know. I thought she'd stayed behind in England.'

Tim shook his head. 'No. There's just Dad and me now.' He stood up, prowling around looking at everything in the office, touching things here and there. 'Dad's had a pretty rough deal, you know, and I just want him to be happy again. I remember he used to be, ages ago, when we lived in Brisbane.'

He turned and walked back to the desk sitting down once more. 'I was only a kid but I knew my mother was sick, she was for as long as I can remember. Dad told me she was an alcoholic and that it was like a kind of sickness.' He sighed. 'Mum and Dad never got on and I guess I didn't see much of Dad back when my mother was alive. Every time he came home Mum would go on an even bigger binge and she'd shout at him and throw things. I heard my grandmother tell Dad once not to come, but he said he wanted to see me.' Tim looked down at his hands. 'My grandmother looked after me most of the time.'

Yvie sat in her chair unable to move, wanting to scream at Tim not to tell her, she didn't want to know. It was easier when she'd imagined he'd gone back to his loving wife and family. She understood that. But to learn that he'd gone back to the situation Tim was describing ... Yvie's heart constricted painfully.

'I guess I kind of held it against Dad, too. I knew Mum was worse when Dad came home. I was mixed up. I wanted Dad to be there, but I thought he was cruel to her or something. But he wasn't. Mum just couldn't help herself.'

'Oh, Tim, I'm sorry,' Yvie said quietly.

He nodded. 'Just before my grandmother died she explained it all to me, how my mother had always had a drinking problem even when she was a teenager. She hid it from Dad for ages. Then Dad kept going off all over the world and Mum couldn't take that. I suppose having me didn't help, either.'

'Oh no, Tim. Your father cares for you a great deal, believe me.' Yvie swallowed the lump in her throat.

'But I've given him a pretty bad time too,' he admitted. 'I . . . after Mum died I think I went a bit crazy. I hung around with some guys at school, real rough types, and I skipped classes and did stupid things. I was pretty foolish all around.'

'But you're not now,' Yvie tried to reassure him. 'Your father knows that.'

Tim nodded. 'The thing was that I really liked school. I always did. But Dad's helping me and I'm really getting back into my work.' He gave a crooked grin. 'That's why he's taking me on this tour this afternoon.'

'And you'll enjoy that.' Yvie smiled and Tim's glance went to the stack of papers on her desk.

'I'm not exactly letting you get on with your work, am I?' he asked.

'Not exactly. But I don't mind.'

'I'll get back to my book. And, Yvie, I'm glad I told you. I wanted you to know.'

Yvie nodded, not trusting herself to speak. Oh Tim, if you only knew how much food for thought you've given me.

When Josh returned Yvie was engrossed in a manuscript and Tim was reading his book. They both looked up as the door opened.

'Ready to go shopping?' he asked Tim after his glance had gone from Yvie to his son.

'Sure, Dad.' Tim stood up. 'Where are we picking up the tour?'

'In the city after lunch,' Josh told him.

'Maybe Yvie could have lunch with us,' Tim suggested.

'Thanks all the same, Tim, but I'll be busy here,' she hastened to tell him. 'I'll just have a quick sandwich.'

'Okay. Well, we'll see you later.' Tim lifted his hand in a half wave and Josh nodded coolly and they were gone.

She mustn't allow herself to dwell on Tim's confidences. When Josh said goodbye four years ago, did he——? No. She wouldn't think about it. Not yet. Maybe not ever. It would only make things worse. Perhaps he had meant it when he said he loved her. Perhaps——? Yvie didn't know what to think.

Later in the afternoon Dan called her into his office. Both Paul and Abby were there before her and her heart sank. Oh, no. She hoped Dan wasn't going to go on at length. He had a habit of doing that just when you didn't want him to and she only had an hour to finish the rest of her work.

'Join the gathering.' Paul pulled a chair forward for her and Yvie sank into it.

'Right. We're all here.' Dan drew on his long cigarette and exhaled smokily. 'We're going out to dinner tonight. Everybody free?'

'If it's free I'm free,' laughed Paul as Yvie sighed to herself. Really, she could have done with an early night after the trauma of the evening before.

'Josh will be back anytime so I thought it would be a good opportunity for us all to get together.' Dan beamed.

Abby positively glowed. 'Fantastic! Dinner with Josh Graham I know I can handle.'

'And dinner with you two lovelies I can handle,' Paul put in.

'I thought we'd go up to the Peacock Room on the top floor,' continued Dan. 'The food's good and it won't mean crossing the city. It's right on our doorstep.'

'Fine by me,' agreed Paul.

'Good. We'll head up there as soon as Josh gets back. We can have a few drinks before dinner.'

Back in her office Yvie touched up her makeup and brushed her hair. She could only hope that the dinner didn't drag on for any length of time. Tonight she wanted the oblivion only a sound sleep would bring.

The Peacock Room was a relatively large restaurant but intimately set out and furnished. When Josh and Tim returned they rode up en masse in the elevator and spent an hour relaxing in the bar before eating. Abby and Dan kept Josh amused while Yvie was content to sit with Paul and Tim.

Not that she wasn't aware of Josh. She was. With every fibre of her being. And had she been honest with herself she would have admitted that a feeling somewhat akin to jealousy niggled away at her when Abby put her hand on Josh's arm or laughed up at him.

But Yvie knew she had no right to feel possessive of Josh Graham and she shouldn't be feeling this way. All that was in the past. It was ancient history. Yet her stomach twisted as Josh laughed at something Abby said. She wanted to rail against both of them although she knew Abby was an innocent party. Knowing Abby as she did Yvie knew Abby would be acting differently if she had been aware of Yvie's relationship with Josh. Abby would never poach on anyone else's territory.

Yvie took a gulp of her drink and almost choked. She muffled her splutter and her lips twisted wryly. Josh Graham was hardly her territory, if he ever had been.

Then Tim claimed her attention, enthusiastically telling her about his afternoon tour of the city.

'We drove through Chinatown and up to Twin Peaks and over the Oakland Bridge. It was marvellous, wasn't it, Dad?'

'What was that, Tim?' Josh looked across at his son.

'The tour. It was great, wasn't it?'

Josh nodded. 'Yes, I enjoyed it.'

'I took nearly two rolls of film,' Tim continued. 'Hope all my shots come out. Oh, and I collected my other film, Yvie.' He dug in his camera bag and pulled out a folder to show her the photos he'd taken. He grinned as he produced the last two prints.

'This is you and Dad startled and this is you and Dad sort of smiling. Well, you are. Dad isn't,' he added.

Yvie glanced down at the photos and felt a dull flush begin to wash her face. They were leaning close together and Josh's hand clasped her arm, his shoulder brushing hers. Interrupted in an intimate situation, or so it appeared.

Paul took the photo from her fingers and shot her a quick probing look.

The other photo was hardly much better, apart from Josh's studied lack of expression and Yvie's pasted on smile.

'Where was this taken?' Paul asked as he passed the photos to Abby.

'At a restaurant near where we're staying,' Tim told him. 'We went to dinner the other night. It was a great meal.'

At that moment they were told their table was ready so they moved into the dining room. They were shown to a table by the window and Tim was immediately taken by the view. He gazed at the panorama of the nightlit city below them while the adults seated themselves.

Somehow Yvie ended up between Josh and Paul and her body involuntarily tensed as Josh's leg touched hers. She shifted in her seat breaking the contact and then perversely wanted to touch him again.

They deliberated over the menu and then chatted while they awaited the first course. Dan dominated the conversation with his usual style, but Yvie sat all but speechless. She was far too aware of Josh so close beside her, his taut thigh only centimetres from hers.

Once her napkin slid from her lap and they reached down together to retrieve it, their fingers touching. Yvie drew her hand back as though she'd been stung, her heart beating a tattoo in her breast.

And the culinary standard of the meal was lost to her for she hardly did justice to the more than adequate food. Only Dan and Tim ordered dessert and as the unobtrusive band was playing Paul turned to Yvie and drew her to her feet.

'Let's dance off some of that rich food,' he said as he led her through the tables and on to the microscopic dance floor, drawing her lightly into his arms.

'I didn't know you'd been out to dinner with Josh,' he remarked casually when they'd circled the floor a couple of times.

'Pardon?' Out of the corner of her eye Yvie watched Josh and Abby heading for the dance floor. 'Oh. Yes.' She drew her thoughts back to Paul's comment. 'Last Saturday night.' She mentioned the restaurant and told him how nice the meal had been. Funny, now she could recall quite vividly what they had ordered while at the time she'd been unaware of what she was eating.

Paul nodded. 'I spoke to Josh, by the way, about Tim going out to Yosemite with Dad and he's quite keen on the idea. He's going to talk to

Tim about it tonight and phone me tomorrow. I think Dad's hoping to be leaving Wednesday morning.'

'Tim will be thrilled about going and Josh can rest assured that your father knows the area and is used to boys, what with his scout troup and all.'

Paul nodded and swung her around as the music stopped. Yvie studiously kept her eyes averted from Josh and Abby as they left the dance floor and walked back to their table. Dan was talking to a well-groomed young woman.

'Oh ho! Wonder if Dan planned this or it was accidentally contrived,' Paul commented in Yvie's ear.

'Hello. Yvie, isn't it? And Paul.' Arched eyebrows climbed higher and the green eyes glowed at Paul.

'Hi Marley!' Paul smiled back. 'Read your interview with Jane Hilton last week. Not a bad write up.'

'Why, thank you, Paul. I do my best.' Her eyes slid from Paul to Josh and Abby as the other couple joined them.

Yvie sank into her seat.

Marley Peters was a well known journalist who specialised in interviewing famous people. She seemed to be able to obtain an interview where all others failed and she had had many a scoop. Of indeterminable age she looked exactly what she was, an attractive, well groomed, successful career woman.

Tonight she wore an emerald green velour catsuit with high heeled sandals that added height to her already willowy figure. Her auburn hair was piled on to her head and she held a cigarette lightly between fingers that were red tipped to match her lipstick.

'Ah, Josh.' Dan beamed, pushing himself to his feet. 'Come and meet Marley Peters. Marley, this is our much celebrated writer, Josh Graham.'

Marley extended her hand and Josh took it, smiling warmly. They were both charmers, Yvie reflected, as her own hands clutched together under the table. Would she always feel like this when Josh was around? Cut about every time he smiled at another woman. Because she was jealous, she couldn't not admit it.

'I've just been talking to your charming son,' Marley was saying and Tim smiled self-consciously.

Yvie took a steadying sip of her coffee, only vaguely following the conversation.

'I'd be pleased to give you an interview, Miss Peters.' She heard Josh say. 'How could I refuse?'

Yvie's eyes flashed to his face in surprise. Josh never gave interviews. She couldn't remember seeing any articles about him, apart from one very sketchy account of his life after his first book began its meteoric rise, and that write-up hadn't been an official interview, just a dredging up of already known facts. Josh's blue eyes were dancing at some quip Marley made and then they were shaking hands and Marley was moving off to rejoin her friends.

'Thursday afternoon at five-thirty. A bit late in the day, isn't it?' Dan frowned.

'I usually take a break from work about then,' Josh said and Dan nodded.

'Wall, I can't be there at that time. I don't think I can get away from my other appointment by five-thirty so Yvie had better stand in for me.'

Yvie straightened in her chair. What had she missed? She blinked enquiringly at Dan.

'When Marley Peters interviews Josh,' he explained. 'You can leave work early so that you're there in good time to sit in on the interview.'

'That should be interesting, Yvie,' put in Abby. 'Marley Peters is supposed to be a fantastic interviewer.' She turned and winked at Josh. 'And you'll have to be on your mettle. Marley has been known to ferret out every last intimate little secret without any effort at all.'

Josh's eyes slid to Yvie and away again. 'Then I shall have to be on my guard, shan't I?' he replied drily.

It was nearing eleven o'clock by the time Yvie turned into the driveway of the house. A figure stood up from his seated position in front of the garage door, arm shielding his eyes from the car's headlights.

'What the——?' Josh went to climb out of the car.

'It's all right,' Yvie stopped him hurriedly as she recognised the tall thin figure. 'It's Larry.'

She heard Josh's sharply drawn breath as she accelerated into the garage. Larry followed the car inside, dumping his kitbag on the floor and striding across to give Yvie a bearhug as soon as she stepped from the car.

'Yvie! What's the idea of being out on the town the very night I arrive.' He kissed her noisily. 'But it's great to see you, as usual.'

Yvie extricated herself and smiled shakily up at him. 'I didn't know you were coming or I wouldn't have gone out.'

'Doesn't matter, love. I haven't been waiting that long.' He tapped her on the bottom. 'I stopped off on the way here and had a couple of drinks with the boys.'

He suddenly realised Josh and Tim had stepped from the car and Yvie saw his startled expression as his eyes fell on Josh and recognition dawned. Larry's smile faded as the two of them eyed each other, neither making the first sign of acknowledgement.

Yvie stepped in quickly. 'Larry, this is one of our writers, Josh Graham, and his son, Tim. And this is Larry, Larry Dean,' she finished stiltedly.

Josh gave the younger man a cold nod pointedly not offering his hand. Larry's face was equally coldly set while Tim looked perplexedly from Larry to Yvie. Oh, Tim, don't say anything, please, she begged him inwardly. She couldn't face explanations tonight.

'Thanks for the lift back,' Josh said flatly. 'We'll say goodnight. Come on Tim.' He put Tim in front of him and hurried him towards the stairs, leaving Larry and Yvie alone.

Yvie opened the door to her flat and Larry picked up his kitbag and followed her inside.

'What's going on, Yvie? You could have knocked me for six when I saw Graham here.' He paused. 'Are you back together?' he asked quietly.

Yvie shook her head. 'No. It's nothing like that. I've learned my lesson where Josh Graham's concerned, wouldn't you say?' she remarked a trifle bitterly. 'No, Larry, he's just here to work on his latest book. He's now with the publishing group I work for.'

'Heck! I'll bet you were surprised to see him.' Larry watched her face. 'Where's his wife?'

'She died.' Yvie turned away to switch on the kettle. 'Like some coffee?'

'Sure would.' He paused. 'Ah, Yvie. Any chance of you two getting back together?'

Yvie shook her head again. 'No, no chance.' She could feel Larry watching her closely.

'Why not? You were always nuts about him.'

She was not unaware of the faint edge to Larry's tone. 'Oh, Larry, let's drop it. There's been too much water under the bridge since then.' She busied herself setting out the coffee mugs. 'Now, enough of that. Tell me your news. How long will you be here?'

'Only tonight,' he replied. 'Can I use your camp bed, by the way?'

'Mmm.' As she agreed it crossed her mind to wonder what Josh would make of Larry staying here. Well, he could make what he liked of it. He thought they were married, after all. And Larry had stayed over on two previous occasions.

'Thanks. And I have got some news. You'll never guess, Yvie.' He grinned broadly at her. 'I'm getting married.'

'Married? Oh, Larry, that's great,' she smiled at him and meant it.

He nodded and grabbed her swinging her

precariously around in the small flat. Laughing they collapsed against the cupboard rattling the crockery.

'Cindy's a great girl, Yvie. You'll love her. She lives up in Seattle and I met her last time I was on leave.' Larry held her loosely in his arms. 'We're getting married this Saturday and then we're flying home to Australia.'

'Larry, that's wonderful, I'm really happy for you.' Yvie reached up and kissed his cheek.

He grinned crookedly. 'Thanks, Yvie. And Cindy and I want you to be there at the wedding.'

'Oh, Larry, I don't think——' she began but Larry took her hand.

'It's okay, Yvie. I told Cindy all about us. I hope you don't mind, but I wanted things to be straight with her right from the start. And we both want you there. You see, my father's not well enough to fly over here and Mum won't leave him so you're all the family I've got. I'd really appreciate having you there, Yvie.'

Yvie looked at him and fought a wave of guilt. What had she ever done to Larry except almost ruin his life. She owed it to him to go to his wedding if that was what he wanted.

He reached in his pocket. 'See, an airline ticket to Seattle for Saturday. What do you say, Yvie?'

'All right. I'd like to come, Larry,' she agreed.

'Beaut! I'll pick you up at the airport and everything so you've no need to worry about that, and there's a flight back that night or in the morning if you prefer.'

They sat up drinking their coffee, talking about

Larry's plans, Cindy and his family, before going to bed. Yvie was so tired she fell asleep immediately so she had no time to think about anything and in a flash it was morning. She dropped Larry in the city on her way to the office.

'I'll ring you tomorrow night to make sure you don't change your mind. See you on Saturday,' he called, waving as she drove away.

Yvie had barely settled back to her work after lunch when Paul strode into her office.

'Hi gorgeous!' he grinned. 'Just thought I'd let you know that everything's planned. Tim's off to Yosemite with Dad and the boys tomorrow and they'll be back late Sunday.'

'That's fine. Tim will love it. But what about a sleeping bag and——' she began and Paul held up his hand.

'Don't worry your pretty head about all that. It's all fixed. Dad has everything under control. All you have to do is bring Tim into the city with you tomorrow morning and Dad will collect him from here.'

'That was quick work. Do Josh and Tim know about all this?'

'Sure do. I phoned them myself. Need anything arranged? Just leave it to me. And when are we going out for a nice cosy dinner?' he smiled engagingly down at her.

'Paul Rosetti, you're a flirt.' Yvie laughed back at him. 'Now let me get back to work.'

'All work and no play,' he said teasingly as he left her.

Tim was waiting for Yvie when she arrived home that night. He was ecstatic about his trip and eagerly regaled her with the things he was going to see. El Capitan. Bridalveil Falls. He couldn't wait for tomorrow. And he had everything packed already.

'What time will you be leaving in the morning? The usual time?' he asked and Yvie nodded.

'I've been working like a slave all day on my maths,' he told her as he followed her into the flat looking curiously around him, his eyes not missing Larry's camp bed which she hadn't stowed away that morning.

'Did your, uh, your husband leave again this morning?' he asked, shoving his hands into the pockets of his jeans.

'Yes. I dropped Larry in the city. He was catching a plane up to Seattle at lunchtime.'

'Oh. Did he . . . are you still, well, friends with him?'

Yvie put her bag on the table and sank down on to the sofa. 'Yes, Tim. We're still good friends. We always were. We made the mistake of thinking friendship was enough on which to build a marriage.' At least, she had thought so, but Larry . . .

Tim nodded. 'Is he on leave from his ship?'

'Mmm.'

'Will he be coming back?'

'No. I don't think so.' She smiled and was about to tell him of Larry's prospective marriage when Josh's voice called Tim from the top of the stairs.

Tim raised his eyes towards the ceiling

expressively. 'I'd better go. Dad's been like a bear with a sore head all day. I don't know what's bugging him.' He gave Yvie a cryptic look before he turned and hurried out of the flat. 'See you in the morning.'

Yvie remained where she was and she sighed unconsciously. She glanced around the flat. She had always felt so peaceful, so 'at home' here, but tonight her little haven was becoming hollow and lonely.

Josh's face swam before her eyes and she felt a lump rise in her throat. She had loved him so much. She still did. That was the whole problem in a nutshell. She'd loved him four years ago and she'd never stopped loving him. She'd tried to bury her love, and she'd thought she'd succeeded, but, it had simply been lying dormant waiting for his return.

Her conversation with Tim that afternoon rushed back to her and she saw a side of the situation she'd never imagined. Josh with his failing marriage, his concern for his son. She could see now that he'd been faced with making a choice four years ago, a choice she'd mistakenly thought had been so cut and dried.

He'd been using her and deceiving his wife. That was the truth as she'd seen it all these years. Black and white. Now it seemed it hadn't been as clearly defined as she'd imagined it to be. A tear trickled down her cheek. Now that she knew Tim how could she blame Josh for his decision.

She wished she could run upstairs and tell him she loved him still, unburden herself, explain about the baby, their baby, tell him of her hurt at his rejection. But, of course, she couldn't. How much simpler things would have been had they not met four years ago, that their first meeting had been at the airport less than two weeks ago, that their mutual attraction could have grown and . . .

And what? she demanded of herself cynically. That you would have begun an affair which would have lasted as long as his stay in the States, and then been over just like before.

She stood up and angrily dashed the tears from her eyes. Don't you ever learn, Yvie Dean? Don't you ever learn?

CHAPTER TEN

AT dead on five-thirty next afternoon Yvie walked determinedly up the stairs into Josh's domain. She knew Marley hadn't arrived and her first thought had been to wait in the safety of her flat until the other woman turned up before she sorted out Josh, but she chastised herself for being childish. What could Josh do anyway with Marley due any moment?

Yvie tapped lightly on the door, opened it, and stepped up into the hallway.

'Josh?' she called, undecided about walking uninvited along to the study or the living room.

But at that moment Josh appeared. He had obviously just come from the shower and as he stood before her he pulled a light fawn windcheater over his head. He smoothed his hair back into place with his hand and in his dark brown slacks he looked as attractive as he'd ever looked.

Yvie swallowed nervously as he stood back for her to precede him into the living room. She held herself tensely as she passed him, her nostrils quivering at the clean fresh scent of him.

'Thanks for arranging for Tim to go to Yosemite,' he said when Yvie had refused his offer of a drink and sat watching him pour a small scotch for himself. 'I spoke to Mr Rosetti, senior, on the phone and it seems he often takes groups of scouts camping so I'm satisfied Tim's in good hands.'

'I'm sure he is,' Yvie agreed. 'Paul's is a very close family. They always vacation together when possible.'

Josh took a sip of his drink and began to prowl about the room. Tension seemed to be multiplying with each second beneath the cover of their mundane conversation. Yvie wished he'd sit down. He was scarcely helping the situation.

'You're fortunate to have Marley interview you,' she remarked at last when the silence stretched to screaming pitch. 'She really is the best in the business.'

Josh shrugged not meeting her eyes. 'It works both ways,' he said. 'I'm not in the habit of giving interviews. My life, my private life, hasn't exactly been a roaring success story to date.'

He drained his glass, went to pour another and stopped, deliberately setting the empty glass on the counter top.

'It was quite a surprise the other night, wasn't it?' he remarked easily, his face devoid of expression while tension emanated from every line of his body.

'The other night?' Yvie repeated stupidly.

'Your husband arriving back.'

'Yes. Yes, it was.' Her eyes fell from his and soft-footedly he crossed the carpet to stand in front of her.

Yvie's eyes were drawn compellingly upwards, over his long legs, his flat stomach, his broad chest, to meet his stormy gaze, and her mouth went dry. He towered over her, eyes probing into her like searing sabre thrusts, and she drew back in her chair.

But what he would have said she would never know for at that moment the bell pealed and she watched mesmerised as he forced himself to relax his taut muscles before spinning around and striding off to answer the door.

Yvie pressed her hand to her heart to still its racing beat and fought to compose herself before Josh returned with Marley Peters.

This afternoon the other woman was dressed in stylish pants and a full-sleeved blouse of a soft semi transparent material and she was as striking as usual. Her eyes went sharply from Yvie to Josh and Yvie wondered exactly how much those green eyes saw for she couldn't have helped sensing the unleashed tension in the air.

Josh crossed to fix Marley a drink as she sat down opposite Yvie, chatting easily to Josh about his flight over, England, and his impressions of San Francisco, gradually drawing him out about himself in a way Yvie could only admire. Marley certainly knew her job, and she also seemed to be instinctively aware of where not to probe too deeply.

When Yvie next glanced at her watch two hours had passed. Marley also raised her eyebrows at the time.

'Heavens, I have a party to attend tonight as well.' Her eyes went speculatively to Josh. 'Why don't you come along? It's a very casual do and a pretty nice group of people, a trifle eccentric maybe but——' She laughed.

Josh's gaze slid to Yvie and Marley didn't miss it.

'You, too, Yvie, of course,' she added lightly.

'Oh, no thanks. I'm sorry, but I can't,' Yvie declined hurriedly. 'I'm expecting Larry to call tonight so I'd better stay in.'

Marley shrugged. 'Well, how about you, Josh?'

His eyes had frozen when Yvie mentioned Larry and he turned back to smile at Marley. 'Why not?' he said easily.

Larry called later when Yvie had almost finished her solitary meal. She hadn't been at all hungry but she forced herself to eat the food she had made herself prepare. She managed to make the right noises to Larry's bright conversation and she even spoke to Cindy who endorsed Larry's invitation for her to come to their wedding. Bring a friend if she'd like to, Cindy suggested.

Perhaps Paul, Yvie thought as she replaced the receiver. But no. There was no point in encouraging those sort of complications. Paul was very nice and a good friend, but she wanted no more from him or any man.

Except Josh Graham. The thought slipped into her consciousness and she sat down on the sofa and forced back the tears that caught in her throat. They were tears of self pity, she told herself, and wouldn't help in the least.

Somehow it was ten o'clock before she made a move to shower and make up her bed.

A rap on her patio door had her starting in fright. Timorously she crossed the room to flick on the exterior light and peek through the curtains. Josh stood outside, the artificial light turning his hair to silver white.

Slowly she unlocked the door and stepped back for him to enter. Closing and locking the door after him she flicked off the outside light. For the life of her she couldn't say a word.

'Would you believe I forgot my key?' he asked at last, one corner of his mouth lifting in a self-derisive smile.

Yvie's eyes searched his face. Why was he here?

Josh's gaze roamed over her taking in her bare legs, the faded and misshapen football jersey that reached her mid thigh and served as her nightshirt. Then his glance found the turned down bed. His mouth tightened and he turned to take a couple of strides away from her.

'It was a great party, Yvie. You should have come,' he said flatly. 'I counted ten television or movie personalities.'

When she made no comment he turned slowly to face her, his eyes suddenly bleak.

'As I said, it was a fantastic party. Any one of the women there could have graced the silver screen, but none of them held a candle to you.'

Yvie went hot all over. She couldn't have moved to save herself. She could only stare at him, watch him step closer.

'I found myself comparing every woman there with you until eventually I asked myself what the hell I was doing there in the midst of those strangers when all I wanted was to be with you.'

His hands reached out to pull her into his arms and Yvie made no attempt to stop him. Her eyes touched his lips, watched enthralled as they moved closer. And then they claimed hers, possessed hers, demanding yet persuasive, parting her lips with an ease that washed away all conscious thought. It was enough to know that it was Josh that kissed her.

Her arms wound themselves around his neck, her body arching willingly against his, feeling the heated surge of his arousal that sparked an answering fire deep within her. His hands caressed her back, pulled her hips impossibly closer to his hard male contours.

Josh lifted the bottom of her T-shirt, slipped it upwards over her head and dropped it on to the floor, his breath catching in his throat as his eyes fell on her firm breasts. His lips burned a trail downwards to kiss both aroused nipples and Yvie moaned his name, her lips teasing his earlobe.

They were on the bed now. Perhaps Josh had carried her there, or they had walked, Yvie couldn't have told. All that was real was Josh's hard body beside her.

He had discarded his shirt and trousers and she drank in the remembered sight of his nakedness, exalting in his primitive beauty. His lips continued to tantalise her, his tongue teasing each rosy peak of her breasts, his fingers sliding downwards over the flatness of her stomach.

He raised his head to look at her, his blue eyes as black as the deep turbulent seas, and then his gaze slid down over her breasts, her stomach. His fingertips trailed along the scar, barely visible now.

Yvie froze. Her mouth dried and her hands stilled where they moved over his chest.

'You didn't have this before,' he said huskily.

His finger followed the length of the mark once again. 'It's pretty big for an appendix scar, isn't it?' His eyes moved back to her face.

'Yes,' Yvie agreed breathlessly.

'What happened?' he asked evenly, sensing her stillness now, the paleness of her face.

'Nothing,' she said, her thought processes numb as she tried to tell herself to laugh it off. 'It was nothing,' she repeated.

Josh was still now, too, and his eyes probed her, searched down into her soul. 'It doesn't look like it was nothing,' he said quietly.

'What does it matter?' Her laugh sounded strained in her ears and she moved her hands against him again. She had to stop his questions.

His hand covered hers, stilled its motion, and his eyes impaled her.

'It's . . . it was a Caesarean.' The words tumbled out of her mouth.

His face might have been carved in stone and the silence between them was thickly heavy and tight.

'You had his child?' The question was wrenched from him and a wave of pain crossed his face. He shook his head as if to clear it. 'I somehow never imagined——' He stopped and eased himself away from her. 'You had his child?' he repeated, and in her sensitivity Yvie read accusation in his tone.

'Well, I was married to him,' she said cruelly, the hurt twisting inside her to rise like bile.

Josh stood up, unconcerned about his nakedness. 'Yvie, for God's sake!' He turned back to her.

Something snapped inside Yvie. All the pain, the hurt, the loneliness, the guilt, welled up and she wanted to lash out at him, flay him with her nails. How dare he? How dare he? She stood up off the bed and faced him.

'Yes, I did have a child, Josh, a daughter. She was born six months after you left.'

He had paled about his mouth and he looked as though he had taken a blow to the solar plexus. 'What are you saying, Yvie? That she was mine?' His voice was coldly quiet.

'Yes, I'm saying that,' Yvie threw at him. 'She was your child, but you didn't want to know, did you? You'd made up your mind to put me out of your life and you were too busy making the break.'

'Yvie, for God's sake——' He went to clasp her arms but she stepped out of his reach.

'Don't touch me. I can't bear it. I should have had more sense than to let you.' She picked up her T-shirt and shrugged it over her head.

Josh turned away, resting on his hands on the bookcase. Slowly he straightened and turned back to face her. 'Is that why you married Dean?'

Yvie's eyes flickered but she lifted her chin. 'Larry loved me.'

'That's not what I asked you, damn it,' he bit out.

'Larry loved me and I . . . I loved him.' Her voice faltered. 'He was prepared to accept my baby as his.'

Josh flinched as though she'd struck him. Like an automaton he reached down and pulled on his trousers and windcheater. He walked slowly to the door stopping to turn back to face her, his hand on the knob. 'What happened to the baby?' he asked hoarsely.

Yvie stood watching him and she was strangely devoid of feeling. 'I lost her,' she said so softly that he barely caught it.

Josh closed the door gently behind him.

Yvie didn't see or hear from him next day. She really didn't expect to. She went to work and mechanically did her job but she was totally numb inside. She hadn't shed a tear or experienced any emotion since she'd told Josh the truth.

On Saturday morning she made an attempt to drag herself out of her apathy. She had to, for Larry's sake. She packed her clothes for the wedding and tried to fill in the time before she called a cab to take her to the airport.

She supposed she should tell Josh she was going away. Perhaps she should leave him the keys to her car in case he needed to go out or something. She refused to acknowledge the fact that she wanted to see him, to apologise.

Resolutely she walked through the garage and up the steps to the house. She knocked, but there was no answer.

'Josh?'

Only silence replied. Perhaps he'd gone out?

'Josh? Are you there?'

A faint sound came from the living room. Yvie hurried along the hallway stopping in the doorway in mid stride.

Josh sat on the sofa, an almost empty bottle on

the floor beside him and he looked as though he hadn't shaved since she'd last seen him.

'Josh?' she whispered and he looked up scowlingly.

'What do you want, Yvie? Come to tell me some more of your closely kept little secrets? Some more barbs to sink into my flesh?'

Yvie took one hesitant step into the room. 'I came to leave you my car keys,' she said carefully, fully aware of the volatility of his mood. 'I thought you may want to use the car this weekend.'

He shrugged and his lips twisted. 'Well, thanks. And which one of your many admirers will be chauffeuring you around this weekend? Paul? Larry? Someone I haven't had the pleasure of meeting?'

Yvie drew herself together, calming herself. Her stomach was quivering uneasily. 'I'm going away for the weekend.'

'Oh. Where?'

'To Seattle. To a wedding actually. Larry wants——'

His face visibly froze before her eyes. He stood up and Yvie wanted to back away but she was held motionless. He took two steps towards her, anger in every taut line of his body.

'Josh, don't!' The words broke from her and she put out her hand as if to ward him off.

Josh stopped just as suddenly and his flushed face paled. 'Yvie!' It was as though her name caught in his throat, that he had difficulty forming the word. 'Yvie, don't go!'

'Don't go,' she repeated, dazed at the instantaneous change in him. 'But I have to. I told Larry I would and he wants me to be there.'

He turned from her then and his shoulders seemed to sag. 'I haven't the right to ask it of you, have I?' he said flatly. 'You're married to him and I——' He took a deep breath and turned back to face her.

'I wish I could undo the hurt I've brought you, Yvie. God knows I never meant it to cause you pain.' He wiped a hand across his face and his eyes found hers again. 'I feel such a bastard and ... Do you know this is slowly killing me, Yvie, knowing I did that to you, that you belong to someone else.'

The torment in his eyes was too much for Yvie. Slowly the numbness was thawing. She began to feel again. Tears coursed down her cheeks and all the bottled up emotions surged through her.

Josh reached her in a couple of strides, his arms going out to crush her to him, one hand cradling her head against his shoulder.

Yvie cried as though she'd never stop but eventually her sobs subsided and she leant back from him so that she could look into his eyes.

'I'm not spending the weekend with Larry,' she told him gently. 'Larry and I were divorced two years ago. He's remarrying this afternoon and as his family can't be at the wedding he asked me to come. Oh, Josh,' she cupped his face in her hand. 'I love you so much. I always have.'

Some time later from her position on his lap on the sofa she looked up at him with faintly troubled eyes. 'Josh, I'm sorry for ... for letting you think I was still married to Larry and for the way I callously told you about the baby. I guess when you surmised the baby was Larry's I wanted to lash out at you.'

He put his finger on her lips. 'I can understand how you felt, Yvie. I deserved worse for being responsible for putting you through it. Why didn't you tell me you were pregnant?' he asked.

'I was going to tell you the night——' she looked down at the buttons on his shirt, 'the night you told me it was all over between us.'

Josh closed his eyes. 'Oh, Yvie. How can you forgive me? When I set out to find you last year I had no idea—— Even when I knew you were married something drove me to find you, to see you.' He shook his head. 'To ask you to forgive me. . .' His voice caught in his throat.

'No, Josh. Please. Our relationship was a two way thing, I see that now, and I went into it knowing what I was doing. I didn't stop to think about anything except the way *I* felt about you. I guess things just didn't turn out right for us then.'

'They will now, I'll see to that. You're going to marry me, Yvie, and this time I'm never going to let you go,' he said firmly, possessively. 'I love you, and I'm going to spend the rest of our lives proving that to you. You will marry me, won't you, Yvie?' he asked quietly, his eyes holding hers, and Yvie nodded.

'I think that might be the best idea,' she grinned up at him and Josh kissed the tip of her nose.

'Yvie, about my marriage to Renee,' he began.

Yvie ran her finger along his jaw. 'I know quite

a bit about that now. Tim told me about his mother when he stayed with me at the office.'

'He told you?' Josh repeated in surprise.

'Yes.' Yvie sighed. 'I know it can't have been easy for you, Josh, and, well . . .'

'Yvie, I loved you,' he said seriously. 'Believe me, it was the hardest decision of my life. But when Renee's mother was taken ill it brought the whole situation to a head. Renee wouldn't hear of a divorce and she threatened me with Tim. God, Yvie, I couldn't abandon him, an eight-year-old kid, to someone as sick as Renee.'

His eyes bored down into hers. 'I still don't know how I walked away from you. Deep down I prayed I'd be able to sort it all out and come back for you, but Renee went from bad to worse and in the end I couldn't leave her. Immersing myself in my writing was the only thing that saved my sanity. That and Tim.'

Yvie smiled. 'He's a nice young man. Just like his father. He also kept telling me how wonderful you are. Something of a matchmaker, is Tim.' She laughed softly.

'He repeatedly extolled your virtues to me as well.' Josh laughed with her. 'Seems he took quite a shine to you. Just like his father.' He rubbed his hand sensuously up her arm making her shiver with delight. 'Do you know I was even green with jealousy every time you smiled at Tim. So imagine how I felt when young Rosetti appeared on the scene, not to mention your ex-husband. It's a wonder I didn't commit blue murder, or should I say pure green murder.'

'And I have to admit to being very aware of

Abby giving you so much attention. And Marley Peters,' she added.

'I hoped you would,' he said with a self-satisfied smile and Yvie put her closed fist against his jaw. 'Making you jealous was the main reason I went to that party. That and your mention of Larry.'

'Josh, about Larry. Our marriage never even began. You see I couldn't ... well, I was still in love with you, Larry knew that, and I couldn't ... Larry and I never slept together,' she finished, a rush of red colouring her cheeks.

The expression in Josh's eyes spoke volumes and his lips claimed hers almost reverently, his kiss deepening with mounting passion. When they broke apart they were breathing as though they'd been running.

'What's this you were saying about going away for the weekend?' he asked huskily. 'Is there any reason why you have to go alone?'

'I can't see any reason,' Yvie replied lightly. 'Larry's fiancée did say I could bring a friend.'

Josh kissed her lingeringly. 'A lover,' he whispered against her lips.

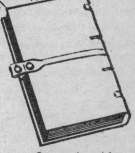

Take these
4 best-selling novels
FREE

Yes! Four sophisticated, contemporary love stories by four world-famous authors of romance FREE, as your introduction to the Harlequin Presents subscription plan. Thrill to **Anne Mather**'s passionate story BORN OUT OF LOVE, set in the Caribbean....Travel to darkest Africa in **Violet Winspear**'s TIME OF THE TEMPTRESS....Let **Charlotte Lamb** take you to the fascinating world of London's Fleet Street in MAN'S WORLD....Discover beautiful Greece in **Sally Wentworth**'s moving romance SAY HELLO TO YESTERDAY.

The very finest in romance fiction

Join the millions of avid Harlequin readers all over the world who delight in the magic of a really exciting novel. EIGHT great NEW titles published EACH MONTH! Each month you will get to know exciting, interesting, true-to-life people....You'll be swept to distant lands you've dreamed of visiting....Intrigue, adventure, romance, and the destiny of many lives will thrill you through each Harlequin Presents novel.

Get all the latest books before they're sold out!
As a Harlequin subscriber you actually receive your personal copies of the latest Presents novels immediately after they come off the press, so you're sure of getting all 8 each month.

Cancel your subscription whenever you wish!
You don't have to buy any minimum number of books. Whenever you decide to stop your subscription just let us know and we'll cancel all further shipments.

"Is it the same with any man?"

"You hypocrite!" Yvie's rush of anger gave her a burst of strength to snatch his hands away from her. "You think you can push me out of your life until it's convenient for you to pick me up again and...." Yvie drew an infuriated breath. "What makes you think I'd wait around for you?"

"You hardly did that, did you?" Josh remarked sarcastically.

"That rankles, doesn't it? That I could forget the great Josh Graham? Well, I did." Her voice caught on a sob. "And I'm not going to let you start it all over again. I'm not!"

Without giving him time to say a word, Yvie spun on her heel and ran out of the study. The tears came in a deluge, and she wept for the past she hadn't left so very far behind. She wept for everything she'd lost.

Books by Lynsey Stevens

HARLEQUIN PRESENTS
497—RYAN'S RETURN
606—MAN OF VENGEANCE
654—FORBIDDEN WINE
692—STARTING OVER
774—LINGERING EMBERS

HARLEQUIN ROMANCE
2488—PLAY OUR SONG AGAIN
2495—RACE FOR REVENGE
2507—TROPICAL KNIGHT
2574—CLOSEST PLACE TO HEAVEN
2608—THE ASHBY AFFAIR

These books may be available at your local bookseller.

Don't miss any of our special offers. Write to us at the following address for information on our newest releases.

Harlequin Reader Service
P.O. Box 52040, Phoenix, AZ 85072-2040
Canadian address: P.O. Box 2800, Postal Station A,
5170 Yonge St., Willowdale, Ont. M2N 6J3